Tales of FEARLESS GIRLS

For Mum and Dad,
who read to me every night
and showed me the power
of stories to comfort,
bring hope, and inspire.

~I.O.

To my grandma Dulce,
who told me the most
wonderful fairy tales.

~A.S.

tiger tales
5 River Road, Suite 128, Wilton, CT 06897
Published in the United States 2021
Originally published in Great Britain 2019
by Caterpillar Books Ltd
Retold by Isabel Otter
Text copyright © 2019 Caterpillar Books Ltd
Illustrations copyright © 2019 Ana Sender
Map and compass images courtesy of www.shutterstock.com
ISBN-13: 978-1-68010-256-7
ISBN-10: 1-68010-256-7
Printed in China • CPB/1400/1773/0421

www.tigertalesbooks.com

TALES OF FEARLESS GIRLS

RETOLD BY
ISABEL OTTER

ILLUSTRATED BY
ANA SENDER

tiger tales

Contents

Story Map

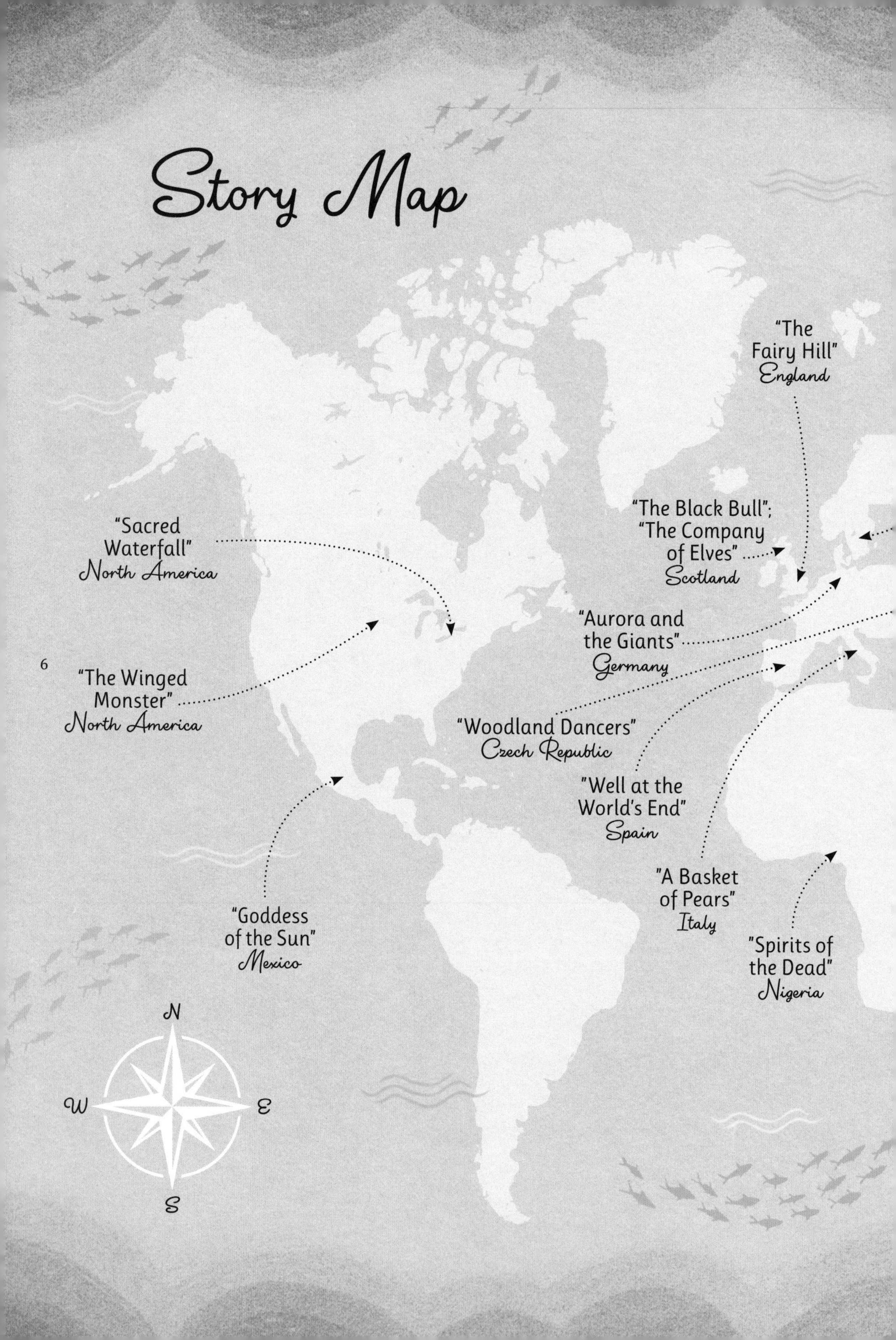

"The
Fairy Hill"
England

"Sacred
Waterfall"
North America

"The Black Bull";
"The Company
of Elves"
Scotland

6

"Aurora and
the Giants"
Germany

"The Winged
Monster"
North America

"Woodland Dancers"
Czech Republic

"Well at the
World's End"
Spain

"A Basket
of Pears"
Italy

"Goddess
of the Sun"
Mexico

"Spirits of
the Dead"
Nigeria

N

W   E

S

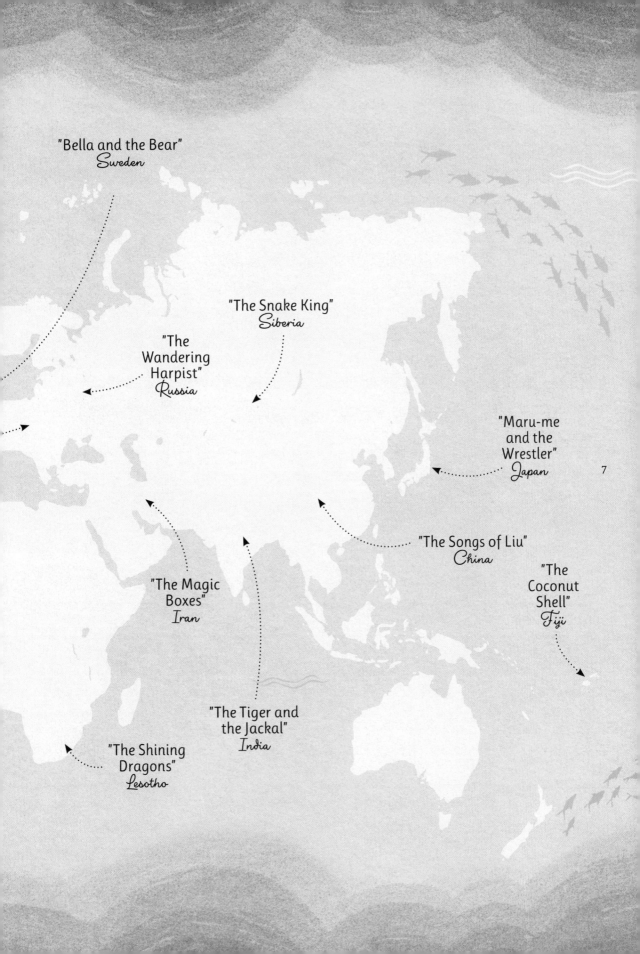

"Bella and the Bear"
Sweden

"The Snake King"
Siberia

"The Wandering Harpist"
Russia

"Maru-me and the Wrestler"
Japan

7

"The Magic Boxes"
Iran

"The Songs of Liu"
China

"The Coconut Shell"
Fiji

"The Tiger and the Jackal"
India

"The Shining Dragons"
Lesotho

Introduction

Fairy tales are stories of daring, magic, and adventure. They spring from our imaginations and can be found in every culture around the world, dating back thousands of years.

Long before humans discovered how to write things down, stories were dreamed up and told aloud. If the audience enjoyed a story, it would be remembered and recounted again. In this way, stories were handed down through generations.

With each retelling, a story might change slightly. In this collection, the tales have been rewritten, but their characters and events stay true to the original versions.

In past centuries, girls were considered weaker and less intelligent than boys. They were expected to behave, stay quiet, and keep their opinions to themselves, while boys were encouraged to be boisterous and outspoken!

Traditionally, the editors of fairy tale collections were almost always men. They included stories that reflected how they thought girls and boys should behave. This meant that the stories passed down to us invariably featured girls who were vain, weak, jealous, or just plain boring!

In many of the classic tales, like *Snow White*, *Cinderella*, or *Rapunzel*, the heroines wait patiently to be rescued by a man, and they are not in charge of their own destinies.

In this collection of fairy tales from cultures all over the world, the heroines are brave, clever, and funny. They don't always say the right thing, and sometimes they make bad decisions, but they're just like real girls. And real girls don't need to be rescued by anyone!

"AURORA AND THE GIANTS"
A story from Germany

After many long years of waiting and wishing for a baby, King John and Queen Mathilde were blessed with a daughter. As was custom, at birth, the little princess was promised in marriage to a young prince named Frederick. The baby had cheeks as rosy as the sunrise, so they called her Aurora, which means "dawn."

Close to the castle was a mighty river. Its emerald water flowed around graceful bends and glittered with promise on sunny days. The river was so wide that the far shore could rarely be seen from the castle. On very clear days, one could make out a carpet of enormous trees, playfully referred to as the Giants' Forest. A small island lay nearby, and King John made frequent trips there. It was a magical place where the flowers seemed more vibrant, the water appeared clearer than crystal, and the air was soft and sweet.

One fine day, the king proposed an excursion to the island. He and Queen Mathilde sailed in one boat, and Aurora followed behind with her nanny. Twenty smaller boats carrying the royal entourage came in their wake. After a few hours of peaceful rest on the island, there was an ominous rumble of thunder, and the sky began to bruise and darken. The party quickly returned to their boats, sensing a storm. Sure enough, the rain began, and the wind started to howl; the boats were tossed about like matchsticks and quickly became separated.

The king and queen's boat was the first to reach the shore, and gradually the others arrived in sorry, bedraggled states. Just one was missing – the boat belonging to Princess Aurora and her nanny. Search parties were sent out through the night, without success. When the boat wasn't found, the queen and king, with hearts full of grief, accepted that their daughter had drowned.

But Aurora was alive! The boat had capsized, and her wooden cradle had floated to the far shore of the river. Little did anyone realize that the place they playfully called the Giants' Forest truly was home to a race of man-eating giants!

Tertulla, the queen of the giants, found Aurora in her cradle on a stony beach. At first, Tertulla thought she had found a tasty snack. But as she lowered her huge head to look at the baby, Aurora stopped crying and smiled. This smile spread a blanket of warmth through Tertulla; she fell in love with the child, and from that day forth, treated Aurora as her own daughter. Tertulla's husband and her eight sons were forced begrudgingly to accept the baby as part of the family.

Aurora grew to love Tertulla dearly but felt no affection for the other mighty residents of the Giants' Forest. She remembered nothing of her past, believing that she was an orphan who had been taken in by the giants. Tertulla's greatest wish was for Aurora to marry her youngest son, Oglu, but the poor girl could think of nothing worse; he was brutish and had no kind words for anyone.

Aurora lived in a small hut by the shore of the river. There, Tertulla taught her the art of magic and even told Aurora where she kept her precious wishing cap. She told the girl firmly that the cap was only to be used in dire circumstances.

Aurora loved to wander in the forest; she felt safe there, as if enveloped in a protective cloak of leaves. One day, she came across a cave. Happily, she filled it with flowers, moss, and animal skins, transforming it into a magical grotto. Aurora decided that on the day of her wedding to Oglu, she would escape to this secret hideaway.

A fierce storm had been raging around the forest, and Aurora found a shipwreck on the shore. As she drew near to the water's edge, she observed a man, pale as milk and hardly breathing. She crouched close to him, and to her delight, he coughed up a stream of water and sat up! Aurora knew that she must hide the man, or else the giants would find and eat him. Seizing his hand, Aurora hurried to her secret cave.

12

Although they didn't speak the same language, Aurora managed to impress upon the man the danger that he was in and that he must stay in the cave. After she had gone, the man looked around. His hand fluttered idly over a chain of daisies, and he noticed a ribbon hanging beneath it, discolored with age. He picked up the ribbon and was astonished to see the name of his long-lost betrothed, embroidered in beautiful gold lettering. The man was none other than Prince Frederick, promised in marriage to Princess Aurora at birth.

Meanwhile, Aurora had gone to find the wishing cap. Her wish was to speak the same language as the man, and when she returned to the cave, they were able to converse! Frederick explained who he was, and told Aurora about her past. At first she didn't believe him, but gradually she felt some fleeting memories stir as he addressed her by her given name.

All of a sudden, they heard Tertulla's booming voice echo through the forest. Aurora fled back to her hut and found the giantess waiting there.
"Oh, there you are, Aurora. Tomorrow you will be married to Oglu.

I won't hear any more excuses! It is decided."
Tertulla swept out of the hut, leaving Aurora to cry herself to sleep.
In the morning, she overheard Oglu telling one of his brothers that he
had found a man asleep in the forest and planned to sacrifice him at
their wedding. Aurora went to Oglu at once saying, "I will accept you
as my husband if you grant me this request – that I be allowed to take
charge of the prisoner until his death."

The brutish Oglu agreed, and Frederick was immediately released into
Aurora's hut, bound in chains. She told him to play along, and all day
she treated him so badly that the giants suspected nothing.

That night, just as Aurora was unlocking Frederick's chains, Tertulla
appeared. Pretending not to have noticed, the giantess said, "Child,
you must bring our prisoner to sleep in the men's quarters."
But Aurora suspected Tertulla's cunning and remained one step
ahead of her....

Once Frederick was lying down and Tertulla had left the room, Aurora
lifted a stone crown from the head of one of Tertulla's sleeping sons
and laid it next to Frederick's head. These crowns were worn at all
times by the male giants. With a quick squeeze of Frederick's hand,
Aurora ran back and spent a sleepless night in her hut.

In the morning, she was woken by a deafening howl of grief and
rage. In the night, the queen of the giants had entered her sons' dark
bedchamber and run a hand along the line of sleeping heads. When
she found the crownless head, she plunged a dagger into his heart
thinking it was Frederick. By morning, Frederick had left, and Tertulla
realized with horror that she had killed her own son by mistake.

As soon as she could, Aurora snatched up the wishing cap and flew to
her cave on nimble feet. With great relief she found Frederick there,
pale and cowering. They hugged, and Frederick began to cry, but
Aurora pulled out the magical wishing cap: "Don't cry Fred; I'll get
us out of here. Take my hand."

She wrapped the cap around their clasped hands and wished harder than she ever had before to escape the wretched forest forever. They felt themselves lifted into the air before landing with a gentle bump on mossy ground. Sweet-smelling orange trees grew around them, and a waterfall spilled into a pool of crystalline water.

Back in the Giants' Forest, Tertulla was looking for her foster daughter.
  "Aurora," she called. "Where are you?"
  "I'm here by the fireside," the girl answered.
Tertulla went over to the hearth, but there was no sign of her. Clever Aurora had used her magic to charm a rose bush to answer in her own voice!

The giantess searched everywhere. Realizing at last that Aurora was gone, Tertulla went to find the wishing cap, but of course it wasn't there! She, too, now feared for her life, as her sons were wild with rage over the death of their brother. Her only chance of escape was a pair of fairy boots. These magical shoes allowed her to cover a mile in one stride; wearing these, Tertulla left the Giants' Forest behind in no time.

Aurora and Frederick had been sleeping but were woken by booming thuds that made the ground shudder. In fright, Aurora used the wishing cap to change herself into a peach tree and Frederick into a bee. The cap hung on one of Aurora's boughs, and as Tertulla raced by, it was caught in the wind and carried away. Poor Aurora and Frederick were trapped, with no way of wishing themselves back!

The cap landed near a girl who was out walking. Quietly, she folded it into her pocket and approached a luscious peach tree. As she reached to pick a peach, she was stung by a bee. Not once, not twice, but three times! Angrily, she pulled a leaf off the tree to shoo the bee away, and to her surprise, the leaf began to bleed. She suspected an enchantment and threw the cap into the tree. Immediately, it transformed back into Aurora, and Frederick's body burst out of the bee.

The lovers were safe at last. They found their way home and were welcomed back with tears of joy. On the day of Aurora and Frederick's wedding, the doors crashed open to shouts of fright. It was Tertulla! The giantess approached Aurora with tears in her eyes.
  "Dear daughter, I'm so sorry for all the hardship I have caused. Please let me live out the rest of my days here, close to you, who I love more than anyone."
They embraced, and all was forgiven.

Eventually, Aurora inherited the crown and ruled as a wise and gracious queen. She never forgot her past and showed special kindness to orphans. The castle became a home for waifs and strays, cared for by Tertulla with love and tenderness.

"THE BLACK BULL"
A story from Scotland

*L*ong ago, in the land of Norroway, there lived a lady and her youngest daughter, Jessie. Her older daughters had both left to seek their fortunes. Aileen, the eldest, had left in a coach pulled by six black horses, while Dorothy had been picked up by a carriage pulled by four white ponies. Jessie's mother was anxious that her youngest daughter should stay with her. But Jessie had other ideas....

She was not happy to have been left alone with only her mother for company. Jessie made up her mind to find her fortune, just like her sisters. With a heavy heart, her mother baked Jessie a loaf of bread, roasted her a slice of meat, and wished her luck in the wide world.

16

Jessie went to the house of a well-known witch, who told her to stand at the back door and watch the road. On the first day, Jessie watched and waited, but nothing came. The second day passed in the same way. On the third day, Jessie was ready to give up hope when she spotted an enormous black bull charging along the road.
  "Missus!" she shouted. "There's a black bull coming this way!"
  "Well, then, it must be for you," said the old woman.
 The bull stopped abruptly, and Jessie climbed onto his broad back.

After traveling for some time, Jessie began to feel hungry.
  "Drink from my left ear, and eat from my right," said the bull.
To her amazement, when she leaned down, Jessie found clear water flowing from the left ear and was able to pluck bread and cheese from the right.

They continued their journey until dusk had seeped like ink through the sky. Presently, a large castle loomed into view.
  "This will be our first stop," said the bull.

After a gracious welcome from the castle's inhabitants, Jessie spent the night in a four-poster bed hung with velvet drapes. In the morning, she was taken into an elegant parlor. The lady of the castle entered and presented Jessie with a shiny red apple, saying, "This is for you, dear girl. Break it open when you're in need, and it will bring you help."

Two more days and nights passed in the same way. Jessie and the bull traveled for hours, and just as Jessie was beginning to tire, a stupendous castle appeared as if out of nowhere. At the second castle, she was given a perfect pear, and at the third, a magnificent purple plum. Each time, Jessie was told to keep the fruit until she needed help.

On the fourth day, they found themselves in a deep, dark valley. The bull came to a halt and told Jessie to dismount. He motioned to a large, flat stone. "Here you must wait for me. Do not move a muscle while I am gone, or I'll never find you again. I'm going to fight an old enemy; if your surroundings fade to blue, then you'll know I have beaten him; if they turn red, it means that I have been defeated."

Jessie stayed perfectly still for a while, but when her surroundings turned blue, she jumped up excitedly, forgetting the bull's command. When the bull returned, he was unable to see Jessie, or she him, and he departed sadly. As the light began to fade, Jessie realized what she had done and despondently began to trudge away from the valley.

Soon Jessie came to a glass hill. She tried to climb it but kept slipping back down. In tears, she walked around the hill's edge until she came to a blacksmith's cottage. Jessie begged the smith to help her. He promised that he would if she agreed to work for him for seven years.

>≪≪≪≪

At the end of the seventh year, the smith gave Jessie a pair of iron shoes with soles covered in spikes. Wearing the special shoes, she was able to climb the glass hill with ease. She slid down the other side and arrived at the house of a washerwoman.

The washerwoman and her daughter were trying desperately to wash bloodstains out of a knight's clothes. Whoever succeeded would become his wife. When Jessie tried, to everyone's surprise, the stains came out at once! But the wily washerwoman lied to the knight and told him that her own daughter had removed the stains. The wedding day was set, but Jessie felt sure that fate had brought her there for a reason. She was determined to save him from this sham marriage.

Suddenly, Jessie remembered the enchanted fruit! She broke the apple open and out spilled a heap of silver. Jessie decided to bribe the washerwoman's daughter to put the wedding off by a day. She felt sure that if she could just speak to the knight alone that evening, everything would be all right.

The daughter was easily bribed, but her sly mother overheard everything and prepared a sleeping potion for the knight. When Jessie arrived in his room, she was unable to rouse him. Frustrated, she broke open her pear. Out of it fell a heap of gold! She bribed the daughter again, but the washerwoman foiled her plan with another sleeping potion.

The knight woke feeling so groggy that he became suspicious. That evening, when the washerwoman offered him the usual drink, he poured it out. Meanwhile, Jessie had broken open her plum. It contained a collection of precious jewels, which as a last resort, she offered to the daughter for one final attempt with the knight.

This time, when Jessie arrived, the knight was up and pacing around. He was astounded to see Jessie, but she quickly told her tale. The knight called off his marriage at once. He was filled with admiration for Jessie, and who could blame him? She was adventurous, brave, determined, and obstinate – all the best traits.

"THE MAGIC BOXES"
A story from Iran (Persia)

There was once a Persian merchant with three daughters named Razia, Fawzia, and Nazneen. One day, the merchant told the girls that he would be making a pilgrimage. They asked him to bring them back presents: diamond earrings for Razia, a diamond pin for Fawzia, and a pink pearl for Nazneen. The merchant promised that he would not return empty-handed.

After his pilgrimage, the merchant went shopping for his daughters. He found the diamond earrings and pin without trouble, but try as he might, could not see a pink pearl anywhere. Tired and irritable, he gave up and boarded the next boat to Persia. The departure time came and went, but the ship did not budge from the harbor. *What on Earth is going on?* thought the merchant, annoyed. Just then, the captain made an announcement: "One of you has made a promise that you have not fulfilled. You know who you are. Until you have carried out your promise, this ship will not sail."

The merchant reddened and crept off the ship to look for the pearl again. Hours passed, and he was almost at his wits' end when he came across an old man, who gave him some advice: "Stop looking for an object. The pink pearl is a man – the son of the king!"

The merchant set off for the palace to meet with the "Pink Pearl" prince himself. He listened to the merchant's tale, and although he refused to accompany him back to Persia, the prince did feel some sympathy for the father, who had gone to such great lengths to find him.
  "Here, take these three boxes back to your daughter," he said.

Aboard the ship again, the merchant waited with bated breath. This time, it took to the water like a fledgling duck. When he arrived home, the merchant shoved the boxes roughly at Nazneen.

"Wretched girl, you caused me great trouble with your ridiculous demand. Take these boxes and leave my house forever!"

Grief-stricken, Nazneen walked for miles. Arriving at an open plain, she threw herself down and stared moodily at the boxes that had brought her so much distress. Wondering what lay inside them, she pried open a lid and was met with the most wondrous sight....

A glinting marble palace soared from the box and stood before her. Nazneen rushed to open the next box and was greeted by a parade of maidservants! Before she could utter a word, they had lifted her up and carried her into the palace. Nazneen wandered dreamily through the fabulous rooms and galleries, feeling like a real princess.

The following day, Nazneen carefully lifted the lid of the final box. Out of it flew an elegant bridge, and over the bridge rode the Pink Pearl prince on a huge stallion. Nazneen led him to the palace, and they soon became inseparable. One day, the prince said, "Nazneen, I ask just one thing of you. Please, never shut the lid of the third box while I am on the bridge. If you do, I shall die."
Nazneen gave him her word.

21

Meanwhile, Nazneen's sisters had not forgotten her. They set out to find her, and in time, a marble palace glimmered into view. The sisters decided to seek rest there. Imagine their surprise on opening the gates only to find Nazneen there, filling a basket with pomegranates!

The sisters embraced and spent the evening reclining in luxury. They took baths in an enormous tub filled with scented water and floating flowers, before being treated to a delectable feast. At last, the girls were led to their bedrooms, where they slept on the finest silk sheets.

The next morning, Razia and Fawzia went off to explore. Soon they came across three boxes. Two were open, but the third was shut.

Fawzia opened the box, but finding it empty,
closed the lid and thought no more of it.
That evening, the sisters headed home,
laden with gifts.

A few days later, Nazneen opened the box, but now no
bridge appeared, and nor did her beloved prince. With
horror, she realized that one of her sisters must have closed
the box while the prince was on the bridge. Tearfully, Nazneen
ran out of the palace, at a loss for what to do. Two birds twittered
overhead, and as Nazneen could understand bird language, she
heard every word: "There is a demon at the foot of this tree. The oil
from his hair will help the Pink Pearl."

Nazneen crept toward the tree, and without hesitation, she killed the
demon and plucked three hairs from its head. She journeyed to the
palace of the Pink Pearl and stood outside the gates, calling, "I can
cure all ills. Whatever your malady, I have a remedy."
Immediately, the queen rushed out shouting, "Please! Come quickly,
doctor – my son is gravely ill, and we've tried everything to save him!"

The Pink Pearl lay pale and drawn, barely breathing. Nazneen hastily
rubbed the demon's oil onto his temples, and the prince began to stir!
His parents were so overjoyed that they offered Nazneen anything her
heart desired for a reward. She asked for the betrothal ring and
a necklace, which the king and queen gave gladly.

Nazneen hurried back to her palace as fast as she could to open the
third box. This time, the bridge appeared with her dear prince riding
over it! When Nazneen told him all that had happened, the prince was
amazed by her wit and bravery, and they decided to stay together in
their palace. The Pink Pearl took to avoiding bridges wherever possible,
and Nazneen, for her part, never closed the lid on anything ever again!

"SPIRITS OF THE DEAD"

A story from Nigeria

Once upon a time there were two cities. One was called Ife and the other Ile-Igbo. Between these two places was a dense forest, and neither city knew of the other's existence. One day, while out hunting, a man from Ile-Igbo lost his way in the forest. Minutes turned to hours, and hours into days....

The hunter had almost given up hope when he suddenly emerged from the trees. Before him was Ife, a mysterious place that he had never seen before. He rested for a while on the outskirts, watching this strange new city. Then, excited by his discovery, he managed to find his way back through the forest to Ile-Igbo.

On his return, the hunter went to find the ruler of Ile-Igbo, known as the oba. He told the oba what he had seen, and people were sent to check whether his story was true. When they came to the edge of the forest and saw Ife for themselves, they noticed with envy the lush fields and gardens, the busy market, and the storehouses filled with food.

They returned and reported their findings to the oba. He mulled things over and began to feel indignant. Why should Ife be doing so well while Ile-Igbo was struggling to feed all its people? It wasn't fair. He devised a plan with his councillors. An expedition would be sent to raid Ife and steal food. Instead of arming the people with weapons, they would dress them up as Egungun – spirits of the dead.

On the appointed day, the chosen people dressed up. They wore frightening masks and bright costumes. Some carried clubs or sticks, others attached arms that hung to their knees, and a few wore gloves that made their fingers look long and grasping. The disguises were so effective

that even the people of Ile-Igbo felt rather scared.

The Egungun marched through the forest. When they reached the edge of Ife, they waited for the signal from their leader. When he stamped his foot, the group began to wail and warble in weird voices. They charged into the city, spinning and leaping, wriggling and twirling, twitching and shuddering. The Egungun were an awful sight to behold.

The people of Ife clamped their hands over their ears and ran away as fast as they could, truly believing that they were being visited by messengers from the dead. Once the inhabitants had fled, it was easy for the Egungun to loot the city. They loaded themselves up with as much food as they could carry and strode triumphantly back to Ile-Igbo, where they were greeted as heroes.

Soon, the stolen food began to run out, and the oba ordered another raid on Ife. The raids became a regular feature of life in Ile-Igbo, and the people began to completely neglect their own fields and gardens, relying only on the pilfered food.

25

‹‹‹‹‹

Ife was now in a desperate state. It couldn't produce enough to feed two cities, and its people were going hungry. Most of them grudgingly accepted their fate, but one bright young woman named Moremi was suspicious. She went to the hut of their oba armed with questions.

"Please listen to me, Oba. Something is not right here. If the spirits are dead, then why do they need food? We don't know where the Egungun come from, or where they go, because we run away as soon as we hear their dreadful moans. I volunteer to stay in Ife next time they come and find out more about them."

"You foolish girl. Don't you know that women are not permitted to look at the Egungun?" said the oba. "If you stay in Ife, you will die." But Moremi stood firm; she believed in herself and refused to take no for an answer.

"I am not afraid," she said stoutly. "If things continue in this way,

we will all die. Something must be done."

A few days later, the Egungun returned. While the rest of the city ran screaming into the forest, Moremi sat bravely in her hut and waited. When the Egungun found her, they were confused. Not knowing what else to do, they carried her back to Ile-Igbo with the loot.

Moremi became a prisoner. At first, she was watched closely and guarded. Eventually she became friendly with the people of Ile-Igbo, and they began to forget that she wasn't one of them. But Moremi never forgot. She bided her time and gradually learned about the deceitful disguises that were bringing ruin to Ife. One night, Moremi decided it was time for action. Dressing quickly, she escaped her compound by cover of dark.

Moremi spent many long days trudging through the forest. At night, she slept in trees to keep out of the path of wild animals. At last she arrived back in Ife. The community was amazed to hear her incredible report of the city of Ile-Igbo and their terrible behavior. Right away, they hatched a plan for revenge....

The next time the Egungun appeared, Ife was ready – they did not flee. Instead, they lay in wait. The Egungun spread through the city as usual, but this time, as they approached the entrances of the houses and granaries, the people of Ife leaped out with flaming torches, screeching and bellowing ten times louder than the Egungun. The invaders were terrified and ran away as fast as they could, while the people of Ife waved their torches and jeered at their retreating backs.

There was a huge festival in Ife, and Moremi was celebrated and honored for her great bravery and resolve. As for those devious Egungun, they well and truly learned their lesson and were never seen again on Ife's side of the forest.

"THE WANDERING HARPIST"
A story from Russia

Long ago, in a distant part of Russia, there lived a czar and a czarina. One day, the czar decided to make a trip to the Holy Land. He liked fine things, and the carriage he traveled in was painted a rather ostentatious red with gilt edges. Unfortunately for the czar, this made him quite noticeable....

The king of the Holy Land was known as the Accursed King and was renowned for his cruelty. He was a vain man and loved to be in the spotlight. When he heard about the ostentatious czar, who was garnering so much attention, he immediately ordered that the man be captured.

The Accursed King treated the czar very badly. At night, he was chained to the wall and forced to sleep standing up. During the day, the Accursed King forced the czar's head into a horse collar and made him pull a plow as though he were an ox.

The czar was distraught. He knew that his wife would be worried about him, and decided that he must get word to her. He bribed a guard with some gold coins that he had hidden in a purse around his waist, and the guard brought him pen, ink, and paper, promising to send his letter.

My sweet wife,
You are probably wondering what on Earth has happened to me. Do not fret, I am alive but in dire circumstances. The Accursed King has imprisoned me. You must come to save me as soon as possible.
From your loving husband

The czarina received this letter and wrung her hands in despair. She spent a sleepless night, tossing and turning and racking her brain.

By morning, she had a plan....

In her spare time, the czarina liked to play the *gusli*, a small, harp-like instrument. Through hours of practicing, she had become good enough to pass for a professional. The plan was simple – she would dress as a wandering musician and undertake the rescue mission herself. First, the czarina cut off all her hair. Then she removed all of her finery, dressed herself in a simple robe, and slipped quietly out of the palace.

The czarina followed the same route as her husband, but unlike him, drew very little attention to herself. When she found her way to the Accursed King's palace, she was faced with two enormous locked gates. The czarina asked the guards to let her through so that she could play for the king, but they sneered at her simple robe and refused her entry.
 "Very well," she said to the guards. "I shall play out here then."

She took out her *gusli* and began to play. Within minutes, the disdainful guards were on their knees in front of her, utterly entranced by the beautiful music.
 "I've never heard anything so wonderful in all my life. The king must hear this!" exclaimed one of the guards.

Without further ado, the czarina was led to the king's courtyard, where she continued to play the lovely, haunting melodies. The Accursed King was rarely pleased by anything, but the harp music touched him so deeply that tears filled his eyes. It had been such a long time since he'd cried that the king didn't know what was happening and shouted for assistance.
 "Why, Your Majesty, those are tears," said a servant, trying to keep a straight face.
The king flushed with embarrassment.
 "You fool. These are not tears! It's sweat – I'm much too hot. Fan me!"

Privately, the king was pleased. He had thought himself unable to cry.
 "Harpist, you play the sweetest music that I have ever heard in my life. I fear if you stop, the color will drain from my world. Please will you stay a few more days?"

The czarina agreed willingly, and after the third day, the king asked her to name her reward.

"Well, it's rather lonely being a wandering musician," she said. "I wonder if I might take one of your prisoners for company."

"Why, yes, of course! Take whomever you please," said the king.

The czarina was taken up to the prison, where she chose the czar as her companion. Luckily, he didn't recognize his wife in disguise! After they had been traveling together for a few days, the czarina released the czar and told him that he was free.

"I can never thank you enough," said the czar. "You won't believe this, but I am actually a czar! Please do me the honor of a visit sometime."

"Oh, don't worry. You'll see me soon enough," smiled the czarina.

It took the czar a long time to find his way home. When the czarina ran out to meet him, he spoke angrily. "Now you welcome me with open arms, but did you shed a tear while I was gone? I think not! If it wasn't for a benevolent musician, I would still be in that dungeon!"

The czarina was unmoved. She was well used to her husband's displays of anger. Quietly, she left the room and went to change back into her musician's disguise before sitting down in the courtyard to play. At once, the czar rushed out and embraced her.

"Harpist! You came! I was just telling my ministers that if I ever saw you again, I would promise you half my kingdom for rescuing me."

With a flourish, the czarina pulled off her robe, revealing the dress underneath. The czar gasped and bowed his head in shame.

"I should have known it was you! No one plays the *gusli* like my wife! Please forgive me. Now, seeing as the kingdom is already yours, may I honor you instead with a seven day feast?"

"That will do nicely," answered the czarina. "But please find someone else to play the music!"

"THE SONGS OF LIU"

A story from China

At one time, there lived a tribe called the Yao. The people lived in harmony with their surroundings in the Kao Yao District of China. The tribe grew grains and vegetables and kept small numbers of animals. They were a happy people, and they loved to sing and dance. When they held festivals, all the surrounding valleys echoed with sweet singing and melodic music.

A young farmer's daughter named Liu San Mei lived near the Yao villages. She was from the Han tribe. Liu wore her hair in a high topknot, and her dark eyes sparkled when she laughed. She was kind and courageous and also a wonderful singer, known for her ability to think up songs on the spot.

Liu was particularly friendly with the Yao tribe due to their love of singing. She learned their dialect so that she could speak to them, and composed many songs for their festivals. The Yao people loved her dearly, even though she was from a different tribe.

One fine day, Liu decided to hold a singing contest. She would begin by singing a verse, and the opponent would sing a verse back. This would continue until one of them ran out of verses. Many people came to compete, but none could match Liu's quick-wittedness.

Eventually, Liu's name met the ears of an old music scholar. He scoffed at the idea that a simple farmer's daughter could be so talented in the art of music and decided to find her and take her down a peg or two. The scholar traveled to Liu's village in a boat weighed down by teetering piles of ancient songbooks.

A young girl was washing her clothes on the riverbank when the scholar arrived. He shouted gruffly, "You, girl! Go and find that so-called singer, Liu San Mei. I am a well-known scholar of music, and I have traveled with my books to compete with her."

Little did the scholar know that the girl on the riverbank was none other than Liu. She immediately sang her response back to him:

> I am Liu San Mei,
> and though scholar you may be,
> my songs are borne of heart and soul –
> they set my spirit free.

The scholar huffed and puffed as he leafed through his books, trying to find the source of Liu's song. A crowd had gathered, and while the scholar became more and more agitated, Liu continued quietly washing her clothes.

The morning wore on, and still the scholar had not replied with a verse. He dug through the piles, sweating and red-faced, tossing books behind him so violently that some ended up in the river!

Eventually, he had to admit defeat and told the boatman to take him home. Liu now became even more famous – people were thrilled that a pompous scholar had been shown up by a country girl.

It was only a matter of time before a magistrate came to hear of Liu the singer. He was a sour, miserly man who loved to go out of his way to ban things that people enjoyed. He disapproved of Liu's friendship with the Yao people and decided that she should be stopped.

The following week, while Liu was working on the farm, a group of young men spotted her and wandered over to engage her in song. They spent hours trading verses under the hot Sun. Passers-by stopped to watch, full of admiration. Liu seemed to have an endless stock of wit and wisdom to draw on in making up her songs. The lanes next to the field filled with people and became completely blocked off.

That afternoon, the magistrate was being carried on his sedan chair to a friend's house nearby. His chair-bearers tried to get through the crowds, but there were too many people. Seeing this blockade, the magistrate stepped down from the chair and called out, "Stop this dreadful singing at once! It is not only improper but immoral. If you must sing, then study first and learn some real songs rather than this nonsense from inside your own head."
But Liu was no shrinking violet and replied:

I don't want verse from dusty books
known only by a few.
My folk songs welcome everyone
and all their points of view.

The magistrate gaped at Liu before clearing his throat awkwardly and hurrying back to his chair. He barked at his chair-bearers to take him away, and the locals cheered to see him go.

One day, Liu met a young cowherd from the Yao tribe who was also a gifted singer. They enjoyed making music together and soon became close companions.

During the Yao spring festival, many people gathered near Seven Star Cliff to sing and dance. As the Sun sank below the horizon and the Moon rose up in its place, the festivities were in full flow.

All of a sudden, there was shouting and pointing. The merrymakers looked up and saw the silhouettes of Liu and the cowherd on top of the cliff. A hush fell as exquisite music trickled down through the air. These breathtaking melodies continued night and day for an entire week.

At dawn on the eighth day, the couple was transformed into stone statues and became heavenly spirits. Liu San Mei was remembered forevermore for her independent spirit and her desire to bring music to everyone.

"SACRED WATERFALL"
A Native American story

Bending Willow lived with her tribe near the mighty Niagara Falls. She was a bright girl, full of joy and a sense of adventure. These positive qualities led to a host of suitors, but they were all unwelcome to Willow; she was already in love with a young man from a faraway tribe. Among the suitors was a chief named No Heart. This spiteful old man was used to getting his way. He was a powerful person, and nobody dared refuse him anything.

No Heart announced their engagement without even asking Bending Willow for her hand in marriage. She felt sick at the thought of living with such a cruel man, but her parents were too scared to challenge the old chief. The day of the wedding was set.

The night before this fateful day, Bending Willow fled into the forest. She ran without knowing where was going, her feet pounding the forest floor. Suddenly she tripped and fell facedown in the dirt. Having fallen, she couldn't get up. Many hours passed.... Willow sobbed until she was exhausted and then lay listening to the roar of Niagara Falls. All at once she sat up – the waterfall had given her an idea.

Willow crept back to her parents' wigwam and took the family canoe. In the dead of night, she dragged it to the river and climbed in. The water was moving quickly, and she sped downstream. Willow mouthed silent prayers to all the gods she knew, begging them to save her.

The canoe started to jolt Bending Willow about; she was in the white water rapids that led to the mouth of the waterfall. Willow could feel the spray, and the roar was enough to drown out her screams for mercy. Onward the canoe hurtled to the brink of the waterfall. Bending Willow raised her arms aloft to give thanks for her short time on Earth, and the canoe went over the edge.

Willow waited for the icy water and the long drop, but instead she felt herself raised up – she was flying on white wings made from clouds! It seemed she would fly straight into the emerald water that cascaded over the cliffs, but at the last second, the curtain of waterfall parted to allow her through.

Bending Willow looked around her in wonderment. She was in a cave, and standing before her was a tiny old man whose white hair and beard were made of mist. He introduced himself as the spirit of Cloud and Rain and smiled kindly at her.

The walls of the cave were studded all over with gleaming white flowers carved from rock. Despite the wall of water that acted as its door, the cave was warm, thanks to an enchanted fire that crackled away in the corner. Cloud and Rain wrapped a thick blanket around Willow's shoulders and led her over to a pile of furs near the fire. He brought her some morsels of fish garnished with a delicious moss jelly.

In the morning, the cave was full of light and dancing rainbows. Willow knew that she was safe from No Heart; he could never find her here. The spirit appeared, his kindly eyes twinkling.
   "Bending Willow, I know your story, and you are welcome to stay here with me. You must not fear No Heart anymore. An evil snake is poisoning the water that he drinks from, and soon he will die. Don't be afraid; I will keep you safe from harm."

Bending Willow stayed with Cloud and Rain for several months. He shared his magic and wisdom, teaching her which herbs and flowers had special properties and how to make medicines. Willow was a quick learner and delighted in her new knowledge.

Her time in the cave passed quickly and happily. When the spirit came to her one day with news of No Heart's death, Willow was surprised; she had almost forgotten about him.
   "It is time to go back to your village, Bending Willow. When you arrive, you must persuade your people to move their camp and live close to me. I will defend you if that evil serpent should dare to follow.

Tonight, I will make you a bridge of mist, and it will guide you home," said Cloud and Rain.

Night fell, and inky darkness spread through the sky. The full Moon hung like a silvery orb and cast a gentle glow over the waterfall. Cloud and Rain summoned spray from the Falls and blew it gently upward. Soon, a delicate bridge of mist formed, and the spirit helped Bending Willow to climb up onto it, calling out encouragingly as she embarked on her journey.

All through the night Willow climbed, until she was back at her village. She was welcomed with open arms by her tribe, and she talked excitedly about Cloud and Rain and the magic he had taught her. The villagers thought she must be crazed from lack of sleep and company.

Willow then started to tell her people about the evil serpent that was poisoning their water.
  "We must move our camp and go to live near the Cloud and Rain spirit. He will protect us," she implored.
After this heartfelt speech, an elder-woman spoke out.

  "That's enough, Willow. We entertained your silly stories about this so-called spirit, but do you really think we'd move from here because of some made-up serpent? This is a good spot with plenty of food."

Willow was distraught but refused to give up. Her family members were the only ones to believe her, and she made sure that they took their water from a spring that was far from the village.

Time passed, and some members of the tribe began to sicken, then died. A few started to follow Willow's advice to gather water from outside of their camp. Soon it became clear that these people were being protected from illness. The elder-woman who had spoken so harshly to Willow called a meeting from her sickbed.
  "I'm sorry, Bending Willow. We should have believed you," she said.

"It is too late for me but not for the others. You must all leave and find a new home."

Bending Willow led the villagers to a camping ground near the cave of Cloud and Rain. They lived there happily for some time before the wretched serpent managed to find them again....

This time, Cloud and Rain was ready for it. He stormed over to the camp with handfuls of enchanted fire. He turned the fire into thunderbolts and then covered the area in a thick sheet of fog. The serpent was blinded by the fog and became confused. Cloud and Rain hurled one thunderbolt after another at the snake. It hissed and spat with rage but couldn't escape. By the third strike, the serpent was dead.

The body of the serpent was thrown into the river, where it floated through the rapids and became wedged at the mouth of the waterfall. Its weight crushed the rocks, and to this day you can see their odd formation, shaped like a tightened bow ready to fire an arrow.

"THE TIGER AND THE JACKAL"
A story from India

Farmer Hardeep was plowing his field when he heard a growl. Turning around, he was horrified to see a large tiger!
"Good day, Farmer," said the tiger. "Are you well?"

Quivering with fear but trying to sound polite, Hardeep answered,
   "Good day, Tiger. I am indeed well."
   "Ah, good. In that case, untie those two oxen pulling your plow," said the tiger. "I am very hungry!"
   "Are you sure about that?" asked the farmer nervously.
   "Oh, quite sure. In fact, the longer we stand here discussing the matter, the hungrier I become. Please untie those oxen at once."

At that, the tiger began to loudly sharpen his teeth and claws. Poor Hardeep fell to his knees.
   "Please, I beg you, let me keep my oxen. In return, I will let you have my wife's cow. It will be much tastier than these tough old beasts." The tiger agreed, and the farmer set off for home.

Hardeep's wife was enraged when he explained what had happened.
   "So your oxen are more important than my cow? And what about all the milk and butter that she provides us with?"
   "Look, Simran," said the farmer. "Without the oxen, I wouldn't be able to plow the field, and we would have no corn. Without corn, there would be no bread. And bread is much more important than your precious milk and butter!"
   "Neither of us should lose our animals," said Simran. "And as you've failed to come up with a plan, I shall have to think of one myself."

Simran sat down cross-legged in her thinking position. After a minute she said, "Okay. Here's the plan. Go back to the tiger and tell him that your wife is bringing the cow, and she is just behind you."

It terrified the farmer to think of returning empty-handed, but as he had no better idea, he grudgingly did as he was told.

When the tiger learned that he would have to wait still longer for his dinner, he snarled and began to pace up and down, swishing his mighty tail and flashing his sharpened claws and fangs. Hardeep's legs gave out, and he wilted to the ground with fear.

Soon enough there was a thudding of hooves, and a hunter rode up. The farmer squinted at him. The horse looked familiar, and come to think of it, so did the clothes and turban. When the rider spoke, there was no mistaking it. The hunter was his wife!

"My prayers have been answered – here is a tiger!" said the rider. "I haven't eaten since yesterday, when I caught and ate three tigers."

Aghast, the tiger turned and ran away. In his haste, he ran right into his servant, the jackal.

"What is going on, Master?" asked the jackal.

"Quick – waste no time. We must run, for there is a wild hunter who killed three tigers yesterday and is on the hunt for another!"

"Wild hunter? You didn't believe in that woman, did you? She was dressed up in her husband's clothes!"

The tiger wasn't convinced....

"I saw her braid hanging down behind the turban!" said the jackal. "Come on – we'll go together. This is a dirty trick to prevent us from eating our dinner tonight."

"But you may be tricking me!" said the tiger. "How do I know you won't run away and leave me to the wild hunter?"

The jackal sighed impatiently.

"Here, I'll tie my tail to yours, and then I won't be able to run away."

The tiger felt much bolder beside his jackal. With tails held high, they marched back to the field. When Hardeep and Simran saw the tiger and jackal, Hardeep leaped up in horror.

"Sit down, you great coward!" commanded Simran.

As the tiger and jackal came within earshot, she said casually, "Oh, you've brought the tiger back for me, Jackal – thank you very much. I am ready for my dinner now."

On hearing this, the tiger wheeled around and fled back toward the forest. The poor jackal was pulled over and dragged along by his tail, howling with rage.

Hardeep and Simran joined hands and danced about triumphantly until they collapsed with laughter in a heap.
  "Tonight, we shall have a feast!" said the farmer.
  "Good idea. We shall eat not only bread, but milk and butter, too!" Chuckling, the two made their way home with their animals following close behind.

"THE COMPANY OF ELVES"
A story from Scotland

Carterhaugh Woods were known to be enchanted. Janet's parents had warned her many times about the dangers that lurked among the shadowy trees. Those who dared to enter would encounter an elf named Tam Lin. He took people prisoner in the woods, only releasing his unfortunate victims if a bribe was produced.

Despite these stories, Janet had longed to visit the woods for many years, as they were planted on her parents' land. She made up her mind that she would venture in to pick a few flowers – what harm could that do?

Janet entered the woods and before long, came across a rose bush hung with dazzling yellow blooms. At once, she began to pick them, and as she plucked the third rose, an elfin figure appeared before her. She dropped her bouquet in fright, and the flowers drifted around her.

  "Who are you?" Janet asked.
  "I am Tam Lin," said the elf. "Why have you entered my woods without my summons?"
  "They are not your woods," answered Janet boldly. "They belong to my parents. Are you an elf or a man?"
  "I'm a man," said Tam Lin. "But the Fairy Queen has made me her knight! It happened one day while I was out hunting. I fell off my horse, and before I had come to my senses, I was in the grip of the Fairy Queen. She dragged me into Elfland!"

Janet stared at Tam Lin, transfixed.
  "What kind of a place is Elfland?" she asked in wonder.
  "Oh, it's fabulous – more beautiful than anywhere else on Earth.

I'd happily stay there forever, but for one small problem.... Every seven years, on Halloween, the elves make a sacrifice to the Underworld. This year, they intend to make an offering of me!"

Janet was brave, and she had a kind heart. Despite everything, she felt sympathy for Tam Lin and offered to help him escape the clutches of the Fairy Queen. Tam Lin was taken aback at first. It had been a long time since he had been shown human kindness, but he soon warmed to Janet. Together, they hatched a plan....

The next day was Halloween – the date that the elves and fairies would ride across the country before making their sacrifice to the Underworld. Janet arrived at the appointed place just before midnight as instructed.

Soon, Janet heard a thundering of hooves. She knew that this was the first company of elves, and that she should let them ride by on their jet-black horses without taking any notice. Janet's heart thudded, but the group of riders went right past without seeing her at all.

When the second company of elves arrived and began to gallop toward her on brown horses, Janet curtsied to them, as Tam Lin had told her to. Once they had passed, she began to feel very nervous. The third and final company to appear would be led by the Queen of the Fairies. They would be riding white horses, and Tam Lin would be at the Queen's side. He'd be riding a stallion, with a starred crown on his head, and wearing a glove on his right hand, but not his left.

After some time, Janet heard a distant rumble – the third company was approaching. As the elves came streaming down the hill, Janet scanned the party and saw Tam Lin, with his starred crown and gloved hand. She clenched her fists and poised herself; she was ready. As the stallion drew close, Janet leaped forward and grabbed its bridle. The horse was strong, but Janet had an iron will.

She seized Tam Lin's hand and tugged him down from the saddle; they fell to the ground together.

"Stop her!" cried the elves, at once leaping from their own horses to surround Janet and Tam Lin. A tall elf stepped forward and murmured an incantation that transformed Tam Lin into a giant icicle. The cold felt as though it were freezing Janet's bones, but Tam Lin had warned her of elf magic, and she was ready to keep hold of him, no matter what. The next spell turned Tam Lin into a burning flame. Janet cried out in agony, but she would not let go.

In desperation, the elves turned Tam Lin into a series of animals. First, an adder that writhed and nearly wriggled out of Janet's arms before turning into a much bigger snake that made as if to bite her, hissing horribly. Next, the snake became a bear that gnashed is teeth and tried to dig its claws into Janet, but she wouldn't let go. The bear then became a lion that gave a deafening roar, but Janet's grip was vice-like.

The elves' final trick was to turn Tam Lin into a red-hot coal, but Janet was prepared. Leaping up, she thrust the burning coal into a nearby well, and immediately Tam Lin reappeared. As he lay exhausted on the grass, Janet tore off her green cloak and laid it lovingly over him.

The Fairy Queen howled with rage and shrieked, "Curse you, Lady! You've taken my most handsome knight! I should have taken out Tam Lin's fine gray eyes and replaced them with dull pieces of wood,

then removed his heart and placed a heavy stone in its place
so that no one could ever love him!"
With that, the Queen of the Fairies pulled her horse around
and charged off with her band of elves following behind.

Tam Lin looked up at the woman who had risked everything for him.
  "Thank you, Janet. You saved my life."
They embraced, and then began their long journey home.

"MARU-ME AND THE WRESTLER"

A story from Japan

Back in the time of the emperors, there was a famous wrestler named Forever Mountain. He was on his way to a competition, where he hoped to impress the emperor. The autumnal air was crisp and cold, but Forever Mountain never shivered. He was much too strong and mighty for that!

Striding on, he found himself by a river and spotted a girl near the bank. She was small and round, and her bright eyes sparkled mischievously as though she might erupt in laughter at any moment. Forever Mountain had a sudden urge to play a trick.

Creeping up behind the girl, he poked her, saying, "Boo!" The girl jumped and shrieked, but quick as a flash, she grabbed the wrestler's hand and held it fast.

"Oh, no! You've got me now. I'm stuck!" joked the wrestler.

"Indeed you are!" said the girl.

The wrestler laughed and started to gently pull his hand away but found that he could not.

"Come now, let go of my hand," he said. "Trust me – you don't want me to pull too hard – I'd injure a little thing like you."

"Pull all you like," replied the girl cheerfully as she began to walk away. "I have great respect for strength."

The wrestler pulled, then tugged, then wrenched his hand, but all to no avail. He tried digging his heels in, only to be dragged along behind the girl, his feet making two deep channels in the ground.

Eventually, he was forced to give up and trot meekly behind. After several hours, Forever Mountain cried out, "Please stop! My hand is extremely sore!"

"You poor old thing," said the girl. "You should have told me you were feeling so tired. Here, I'll carry you the rest of the way."

"No, thank you!" said the wrestler, reddening with embarrassment. "I don't want to be carried any more than I want to be pulled!"

"Oh, dear, let's not be on bad terms; I only want to help you," the girl said sweetly. "My name is Maru-me. What's yours?"

"I am Forever Mountain, the famous wrestler. I was on my way to a competition when I met you!"

"But if you go as you are, nothing will distinguish you from the other wrestlers. I happen to know that the competition doesn't start for another three months. Come with me now, and I can help you to become a truly strong man."

Before long, they arrived at a simple thatched house.

"Here we are," said Maru-me. "And here comes Mother with our cow." The wrestler blinked and shook his head. Were his eyes deceiving him? The woman was carrying the cow in her arms like a baby!

Maru-me explained everything to her mother excitedly. The woman looked Mountain up and down and raised an eyebrow.

"Dear me, we have a lot of work to do. Look how feeble he is! Well, we'll do what we can in three months. Perhaps he can help Grandmother with a few of the easier tasks around the house."

Just then, an ancient old woman tottered out of the house, leaning on a stick. As she walked toward them, she tripped on a tree root.

"Drat! That's the third time this root has tripped me up."

Tossing her stick aside, she grasped the tree and pulled it clean out of the ground. Her daughter took the tree and lobbed it toward the mountain. It sailed through the air and disappeared. There was a thump as the wrestler slumped heavily to the ground. He had fainted.

The next day, Forever Mountain's training began. Every day, the women worked him to the bone, and in the evenings, he wrestled with Grandmother, as she was the least likely to break one of his bones accidentally. Even so, Grandmother was able to throw Forever Mountain high into the air and catch him again.

It was nearing the end of the third month, and Forever Mountain could now pull a tree out of the ground with the same ease as Grandmother. That evening, the usual wrestling match took place, but this time, Mountain held Grandmother down for the first time.

53

"Hooray!" cheered Maru-me.

"Excellent, Forever Mountain," said Mother. "You are finally ready to go before the emperor. Take our cow and sell her. Use the money to buy yourself a weighted silken belt to wear when you wrestle."

Forever Mountain protested. "But how will you plow the fields without your cow?"

The women roared with laughter.

"Oh, Mountain, she is only a pet," said Maru-me with tears of mirth in her eyes. "Even Grandmother is five times as strong as her!"

The next morning, Forever Mountain rose early. He tied up his hair in a tight topknot and bade the family farewell. Hoisting the cow onto his shoulders, he marched off.

Eventually, he arrived at the Royal Palace, wearing his new silk belt. There were many other wrestlers there, boasting of their exploits, just as Mountain had once done. Now, he sat quietly in a corner.

The courtiers sat waiting for the wrestling to begin, trussed up in beautifully embroidered robes. The emperor was bored by wrestling. He preferred books to sports, and he hoped that he could escape back to his library as soon as possible.

The first wrestlers to compete were Forever Mountain against the largest man in all the country. As was customary, the wrestlers stamped their feet to begin the match. The big man stamped first, and the ring shuddered. When Mountain brought his foot down, there was a thunderous boom that made the surrounding towns think a storm was coming. The large wrestler was bounced right out of the ring!

Forever Mountain tried to be gentle during his next matches. He tapped, rather than stamped, his foot and picked up his opponents, before placing them in front of the emperor with a deep bow.

The emperor was thrilled with Forever Mountain. The competition had ended much sooner than expected, and now he could go back to his poetry. He presented Mountain with all of the prize money but made him promise not to wrestle anymore.

Forever Mountain didn't mind a bit. *I shall become a farmer,* he thought to himself. *A much more useful pursuit than wrestling!* He hurried back to the valley, and when Maru-me saw Forever Mountain, she ran over and scooped him up in her arms. Together, they returned to the thatched house, talking and laughing all the way.

"GODDESS OF THE SUN"
A story from Mexico

The gods were gathered together because the world had been destroyed. First, the sky collapsed onto the land, extinguishing the Sun and making the darkness of night endless and unforgiving. Then, the people of Earth were all transformed into fish as a great flood of water enveloped the world.

In the aftermath of this destruction, the gods decided that a new Sun and Moon must be chosen. First to volunteer for the role of Sun God was the Lord of Snails. He swaggered to the front of the crowd with his large white shell strapped to his back, proclaiming loudly that he would willingly change himself into the Sun.

Suddenly, a cough was heard, and the gods all turned to look. It was Little Spots. She was a demigoddess, but the poor girl was afflicted by red sores that pock-marked her entire body. That pitiful cough was fateful, they decided. Little Spots would become the Moon.

She asked for just one condition – that the gods made her complexion fair and smooth once she became the Moon. The gods agreed, and preparations began at once. They built altars on two huge pyramids made of stone. Lord of Snails brought the most extravagant offerings: bouquets of brightly colored flowers, shimmering feathers, and precious stones that shone as though lit from inside. Poor Little Spots could only offer bundles of greenery and a few very small balls of mangy straw.

Now it was time to get dressed, ready for the ceremony. Lord of Snails chose the finest clothes in his possession; rich velvet robes with gold brocade, and a headdress of exotic flowers and feathers. Little Spots only had one dress. It had been white once, but now was gray and stained with a raggedy hem.

A tremendous fire was built. Lord of Snails paced around it, his hands nervously reaching up to adjust his headdress every few minutes. Little Spots, on the other hand, sat quietly and waited, smiling sweetly.

The flames leaped high into the air, crackling and spitting, their light dancing over the faces of the gods who stood solemnly, looking on. The time had come. In order to become the Sun, Lord of Snails had to throw himself into the heart of the flames. He swallowed nervously and clenched his fists. The fire glowed blue and green, and its flickering seemed to taunt Lord of Snails as he cowered before the flames.

The gods chided him angrily, but still he could not muster the courage to jump. Eventually, they called out to Little Spots. Without a moment's thought, she leaped gracefully into the heart of the fire, the same sweet smile on her face. Lord of Snails was humiliated. With a shout, he forced himself to run toward the fire, but again lost his nerve and faltered. Instead of landing in the heart of the fire, he fell clumsily into the embers and turned immediately into a pile of ash.

A mighty eagle appeared and soared over the flames. The tips of its wings were singed and blackened. After the eagle came a jaguar. It bounded over the fire, and as it did so, its blonde fur was scorched with black and brown markings. Next, a hawk swooped through the licking flames, scorching its feathers black. The final creature to sail through the fire was a wolf. Its fur was toasted a pale brown color.

The eagle reappeared, and the gigantic fire divided into two halves. In the eagle's beak was a blazing, golden ball. The eagle glided through the parted flames and soared for miles, before dropping the burning ball in the easternmost part of the Earth.

Following the eagle through the parted flames came the jaguar. It held a glowing ball of silver in its claws. The spotted jaguar raced through forests, jumped over rivers, and scaled mountains before tossing the radiant ball of silver next to the golden ball in the East.

As Little Spots had jumped into the heart of the flames, she became the blazing Sun. The gods seated her on a large, majestic throne that radiated her brilliance. Lord of Snails paid for his cowardice; having only made it to the edge of the fire, he became the paler Moon, destined to be forever outshone.

The Sun Goddess sat on her throne in the East and lit up the sky with the most exceptional dawn ever seen. Peach and purple hues fanned out, and the clouds seemed to blush as her rays brushed over them. At first the gods were thrilled, but four days passed, and the Sun Goddess did not rise or set. She was waiting for the gods to fulfill their promise to make her complexion as beautiful as theirs, but they refused! The world was steeped in perpetual dawn.

The God of the Evening Star became angry and shot an arrow toward her. It missed its target, leaving a plume of dusky sunset colors in its wake. Quick as a flash, the Sun Goddess flew from her throne and began to chase God of the Evening Star. Around the Earth they went, from east to west, and back again.

The Moon followed, but lagged so far behind that by the time he reached the western skies, the Sun had long since sunk below the horizon, ready to light a new dawn on the eastern part of the Earth. Even now, Sun, Moon, and Evening Star continue to follow each other around the Earth. Thanks to their endless game of chase, we experience dawn, day, dusk, and night.

"BELLA AND THE BEAR"
A story from Sweden

Bella was a young princess who lived in a palace on the edge of a verdant forest. The palace yard was beautiful; there were rolling lawns, a large lake filled with white swans, and flowers in dazzling colors. Bella played in the yard all day, but at seven o'clock sharp every evening, her nanny would call her inside for a bath.

One evening, Bella decided that she didn't want to go inside at seven. It was still light, and she could hear the tinkling laughter of her parents, who were entertaining friends. She caught sight of a footbridge over a stream at the end of the yard, and with a quick glance over her shoulder, skipped across into the forest beyond.

Bella ran as fast as she could along a winding path, until she arrived in a clearing. She was so hot by this point that she pulled off her dress, leaving only the petticoat underneath. Folding it neatly, Bella left the dress on a large stone and gazed up at the ancient trees.

   "My, how big and tall you are," she said in awe.

   "We are as old as time," the trees whispered back. "You are not the first little princess to seek adventure in our forest, nor will you be the last!"

   "You are old and tall, but you can't skip and jump like I can!" Bella called as she went running off, deeper into the heart of the forest.

In her haste, Bella tripped on the rutted path and fell down with a heavy bump.

   "Drat these shoes and socks. I shall leave them here until I return." Bella took her shoes and socks off and left them arranged neatly at the edge of the path.

   "That's better – I could run barefoot all day," Bella laughed.

She sped through the trees and marveled at the dappled spots of light that peppered her body. All of a sudden, Bella found herself at the edge of the forest. Before her was an open field, full of wild raspberry bushes. Bella began to make her way through them, eating the delicious berries as she went. When her foot touched something smooth and cold, she reeled back in alarm, but it was only an adder.

Bella wasn't afraid of snakes, and she stuck out her tongue at the hissing adder.

"Aren't you a beauty," she said. "Would you like to dance with me?" Bella began to leap and twirl and the serpent joined in, swaying his head from side to side and wriggling his scaly body.

After a while, the snake slid away, leaving Bella to dance alone. She eventually tired as well, and skipped off to pick more raspberries, intending to save some for her mother and nanny. She picked a big handful but almost dropped them in fright as she heard some heavy steps coming toward her. *Oh, dear! It must be my nanny coming to take me home. She sounds angry*, thought Bella.

But it wasn't Nanny – it was a big brown bear! Bella laughed with delight, for she wasn't afraid of bears, either.

"Hello, Bear! Would you like some raspberries?" She held out her hand, and the bear ambled over and began to gently nibble the raspberries from her palm. When she'd finished, the bear licked Bella's hand with her big, rough tongue, and this made Bella giggle even more.

"What a sweet bear you are, but you must get so hot in that thick coat. Poor thing."

Bella stood on tiptoes and kissed the bear on her wet nose. At that moment, two small bundles of fur came tumbling out of the bushes.

"Oh, what adorable little cubs!" exclaimed Bella. She and the cubs played rough-and-tumble together until they all lay panting. Then, as quickly as they had arrived, the bears darted off, and Bella was left alone.

As she wandered back toward the forest, singing softly to herself, Bella heard a twittering overhead. Suddenly, she felt a weight lift from her head.

"Hey, that's my crown!" she shouted.

"You don't need a crown," answered a crow. "But it will bring my children much joy."

He was perched in a nest, and next to him was Bella's glittering crown.

"Where are your children?" Bella asked.

Four fluffy heads popped up and looked at her warily. Bella clapped her hands, "Oh, do sing for me, little chicks!"

The singing was rather squeaky, and not very tuneful, but Bella didn't mind. She clapped and hummed along with them.

"Keep the crown," she said. "I must be on my way now, as the Sun is beginning to set."

Bella soon found herself at the shore of a lake. Its surface was covered with beautiful white water lilies that glowed eerily in the dusky light. As she was gazing at them longingly, a swan appeared.

"Would you like a closer look?" the swan asked.

"Oh, yes, please!" said Bella.

She climbed onto the swan's back and used her pearl necklace for reins. The swan dropped her off at an island in the middle of the lake, and Bella told her to keep the pearl necklace as a memento. She lay down on the soft, mossy ground, breathing in the scent of the lilies. She almost dozed off, but sat up with a start as she realized that it was getting dark.

"Swan? Swan, where are you?" she called fearfully.

When no answer came, Bella began to cry.

"Oh, dear, oh, dear. Mother and Nanny will be so upset with me. How will I ever get home?"

There was a loud beating of wings and Bella jumped up, thinking Swan was back. Instead, she was faced with an enormous eagle.

"Stop this crying at once," commanded the eagle. "You are disturbing my children, who are trying to get to sleep. It's time you went home."

"But I can't go home!" Bella burst out. "I've come too far, and I can't remember the way back."

The eagle sighed, saying, "Honestly, what a silly thing you are. Well, I suppose I'd better take you back myself. Climb on."

Bella and the eagle were off! As they gained height, the forest below them shrank away, and the trees blurred into a green smudge. The wide and raging river seemed little more than a squiggle of blue pencil.

Before long, Bella spotted her parents' castle, and the eagle began to swoop downward while she shrieked with glee.

64

Bella jumped down from the eagle's back and took off her petticoat.
  "Here, you must have my petticoat as a reward for bringing me home. You can make little jackets for your chicks."

The eagle accepted the petticoat and soared away, while Bella dashed toward the castle. She could hear her parents calling her name.
  "Here I am!" she shouted. Bella's parents scooped her up joyfully and squeezed her tightly between them.
  "Oh, Bella, we were so worried. Where on Earth have you been? And where are all your clothes and jewelry?"
  "Oh, those...." said Bella vaguely. "I'm not quite sure. All I can tell you is that I have had the most wonderful adventure!"

65

"THE SNAKE KING"
A story from Siberia

*L*ong ago, there was a ruler named Kara-Kan, living in the wilds of Siberia. He had one daughter, named Altyn-Aryg. After a long illness, Kara-Kan called his daughter to his bedside.

"Altyn-Aryg. You know I have been gravely ill, and I fear that the end of my life is near. Since you are my only child and I have no sons, I will divide my people and herds of cattle into two and leave you to rule over half. You will not be able to manage it all on your own."

Altyn-Aryg visibly bristled at this comment.

"Why is it that you think I can only cope with ruling half the herd and people?"

"Because...that's just the way it is," said her father.

"Because I'm a girl?"

Kara-Kan sighed with exasperation.

"I am just as capable as a man, if not more!" Altyn-Aryg said hotly. "If you refuse to let me rule over all of your people and herds, I shall leave this land and live elsewhere."

Her mother and father begged Altyn-Aryg to change her mind, but she refused. The next morning, she packed a bag, saddled up her favorite horse, and rode off to a new land. Everybody thought she was crazy, but Altyn-Aryg always had a plan....

After riding for many days and nights, Altyn-Aryg arrived in the land of a well-known hero. She sought out his home and asked to rest there for a night.

"Maiden, I would gladly have you to stay," the hero said. "What is your name?"

"My name is Altyn-Aryg, and I have come here to complete a mission."

"Hello, Altyn-Aryg. I am named Altyn-Kan. May I ask what your mission is?"

"I have taken it upon myself to find the Snake King and kill him. He has a lot of land in his power, and the rulers have to pay bribes to stop him from destroying their people. Too many have already died because of this evil snake, and I intend to kill him, or die trying!" said Altyn-Aryg passionately.

Altyn-Kan was impressed. He bowed his head toward this fierce woman and welcomed her into his home. The next morning, she set off early in search of the Snake King.

Altyn-Aryg rode on through the bleak, desolate land until she reached the edge of a valley. Looking over the edge, she saw the snake immediately. He was as wide as the valley itself, and lay with his enormous jaws open. Altyn-Aryg paled at the sight, but steadied herself and jumped off her horse, telling it to wait for her. The final part of her quest needed to be done alone.

Before long, Altyn-Aryg was standing before the serpent. She was about to enter his mouth when the Snake King's enormous tongue flickered toward her. She leaped back in horror, but his eyes were closed. He was hissing in his sleep. Altyn-Aryg stepped bravely into the Snake King's mouth, trying not to look at his glistening fangs....

It was warm and wet in the body of the snake, but luckily some light shone through his open mouth. As she walked, Altyn-Aryg passed the lost souls of many birds, beasts, and heroes. When the Snake King devoured a living being, their soul became trapped forever in his body. These forlorn ghosts drifted along beside Altyn-Aryg as she strode determinedly to find the Snake King's heart.

Altyn-Aryg knew she was close when she began to hear steady, booming thuds. Her hand tightened around the hilt of her sword.
  "Why have none of you been able to kill this snake?" Altyn-Aryg demanded of the ghostly heroes.
  "A few of us tried, but when our swords struck his heart, they broke in two," a hero replied sadly.

"Oh, dear. Well, lend me a sword. I don't want to risk breaking mine."
A young hero stepped forward and presented Altyn-Aryg with his
sword. Raising it high, she attempted to plunge the sword into the
snake's heart, but on impact, the sword broke cleanly in two. She
looked down at her own sword – it had been a present from her father,
and the blade was engraved with beautiful, intricate patterns.

Taking the hilt with both hands, Altyn-Aryg drew her sword and took
aim again. This time, the sword sank into the heart of the snake like a
knife through soft butter. The snake's jaws snapped shut, and all went
dark. There was a terrifying hiss, then, quite suddenly, light flooded
back in as the snake's mouth opened again.

All of the birds began to soar toward the light, followed by a parade of
beasts, from wolves and bears to foxes and squirrels. After the animals
came the heroes, human again, their ghostly forms filled in. They
shouted for joy and held their broken swords aloft.

Behind the heroes strode Altyn-Aryg. When she emerged from the
Snake King's jaws, the heroes fell on their knees, weeping and begging
her to accept a yearly tribute in payment for their rescue.
  "Heroes – stand up!" shouted Altyn-Aryg. "I won't accept your tribute.
All I ask is that you go back to where you came from and live happily."

When Altyn-Aryg returned home, her parents were overjoyed to see
her. She enthralled them with her adventurous tale, and her father
shook his head in disbelief.
  "Well, my girl, you have certainly proved me wrong! In killing the
Snake King and rescuing the souls of the birds, beasts, and heroes,
you have proved yourself ten times stronger than I ever was."

And so, the Snake King crumbled into dust, and Altyn-Aryg received
her full inheritance after all.

"THE FAIRY HILL"
A story from England

Once upon a time, there lived a king and queen and their two daughters, Kate and Anne. The queen was stepmother to Anne, and jealous of the fact that she was more beautiful than her own daughter, Kate. The queen sought out the hen wife and asked for help.

"Tell Anne to come to my house tomorrow morning. And make sure that the girl eats nothing beforehand," said the hen wife.

The next morning, Anne set off, but grabbed a crust of bread to munch on along the way. When she arrived and asked for some eggs, the hen wife (who was also a witch) told her to take a look in the cauldron. Anne peered in. It smelled disgusting and she drew back, gagging. The hen wife scowled, "Tell your stepmother to keep the kitchen locked!"

The queen saw Anne return looking as pretty as ever and realized that she must have eaten something on the way. The following day, she angrily marched Anne back to the hen wife's house. This time, when Anne looked inside the cauldron, the potion worked, and her head was replaced with a sheep's! The queen clapped her hands with glee. Back at the castle, the queen ran to find Kate. "Look at Anne with her ugly sheep's head! At last you are the prettier daughter."

Kate was outraged by her mother's behavior. That night, she placed a cloth over Anne's head, and the two of them escaped. After walking for some time, they arrived at a different castle.

"Could we spend a night with you? My sister is very sick," said Kate.

"Of course," said the king. "Our son is sick, too, but we don't know why. I'm offering a peck of silver to anyone willing to wait up with him and find out about his mysterious ailment."

Kate loved mysteries and agreed right away. That night, the prince tossed and turned until midnight, then sat up and left the room,

with Kate hot on his heels. He went into the stable, saddled his horse, and rode into the night, but not before Kate had leaped up behind him.

Kate and the prince rode into the woods with his hound following behind. As they went, Kate grabbed handfuls of ripe nuts from the branches and put them into her apron pocket. After some time, a hill appeared ahead. The prince jumped down from the saddle and called, "Open up, green hill! Allow me and my hound to pass through."
  "And me, too!" said Kate.

Inside, Kate was dazzled. Glittering chandeliers cast rainbows on the walls of an enormous hall. There was a long trestle table laden with sumptuous-looking food and drink, and a band of musicians who began to play when the prince arrived. A host of beautiful fairies thronged around the prince before taking turns to dance with him.

Kate shrank behind a pillar to watch. The fairies wore fine, gauzy dresses with holes for their delicate wings. Their long, silken hair flew behind them as they danced on and on into the night. Kate could see how tired the prince was, but each time a dance ended, another would begin. At one point, he collapsed exhausted onto a velvet couch, but the fairies fanned him until he was ready to stand up again. Finally, a rooster began to crow, and the fairies melted away.

On returning to the castle, the prince fell into his bed, paler than ever. When his parents came in, they found Kate quietly cracking nuts.
  "I need more time to figure out this mystery. And for that, I will need a peck of gold."

The following night, the prince and Kate went off to the fairy hill again. This time, Kate sat down in the shadows. A baby fairy was playing with a wand nearby. Two older fairies stood next to her talking: "If only Kate's sister could get three taps of that wand, she would be restored to her former beauty."
As discreetly as possible, Kate began to roll nuts toward the baby, who dropped the wand and laughed delightedly. Quick as a flash, Kate snatched up the wand and put it in her apron pocket.

Just as before, when the rooster crowed, Kate and the prince rode back to the castle. This time, Kate ran to Anne's room and tapped her gently with the wand three times. Immediately, her dear sister's head reappeared. Kate met with the queen that morning: "I'm very close to solving the mystery. If I succeed, you must allow Anne and me to live in the castle."

"Yes, anything," the queen promised. "Just save our son!"

On the third night, Kate sat in her usual corner. The baby fairy was there again, and this time, she was playing with a little bird. A group of fairies nearby was laughing unkindly, saying, "If only the prince knew that three bites of that bird would make him well again!" Kate still had a good handful of nuts. One by one, she rolled them toward the baby, who quickly lost interest in the bird. Kate pounced and stuffed it into her apron.

Back at the castle, Kate roasted the bird and brought it to the prince.
  "Oh, my, what is that smell? I must have a bite of that food!"
  "It's a bird I have prepared especially for you," said Kate.
Greedily, the prince snatched the plate and bit into the bird once,
twice, and then three times. No sooner had he done this than the
color began to rise in his cheeks, and his tired eyes began to sparkle.

A few hours later, there was a tapping at the door. When the prince's
parents peered in, they could hardly believe their eyes. There was their
son, looking as fit and healthy as he ever had. He sat cozily by the fire
with Kate, talking animatedly and happily cracking nuts. The king and
queen upheld their promise to let Kate and Anne live in the castle with
them, and they all lived happily ever after.

"THE COCONUT SHELL"
A story from Fiji

In times gone by, a little girl named Kumaku lived on the island of Rotuma, Fiji. She had long black hair, dark as a raven, and liked to place a bright flower behind one ear. Kumaku had a mischievous streak, and when she laughed, it was impossible not to join in with her.

One evening, her mother asked: "Kumaku, will you please fill this coconut shell with seawater? I need it to cook the rice for our dinner." Kumaku took the shell and darted off. As she skipped past, her mother called, "Make sure you don't go near those spider webs!" But it was not the spiders that Kumaku's mother was afraid of....

74

Giants lived on Rotuma, and it was common knowledge among the islanders that they stretched enormous webs across the paths, hoping to ensnare unsuspecting visitors. Anyone unlucky enough to get caught in a web was eaten up by the bloodthirsty giants.

But as far as Kumaku was concerned, rules were meant to be broken! As she danced down to the sea, she noticed a path strung with the familiar webs. Instead of avoiding it, she changed course deliberately and began to make her way down the webbed path. Being small, she managed to wriggle under the webs, laughing as she went and singing:

> *My name is Kumaku.*
> *I'm going to the sea.*
> *Come and find me, giants.*
> *Approach and carry me!*

As soon as the song had finished, two frightful giants leaped out of the sea and picked Kumaku up. Carrying her on their shoulders, they walked down to the shore in three huge strides and set her down by the sea, licking their lips hungrily.

As Kumaku turned her back on them to fill her shell with seawater, the giants lunged toward her with their awful, clawed hands. But Kumaku had already begun to sing:

> *Whistling wind from Fiji,*
> *Blow with all your might.*
> *Fill the giants' eyes with sand*
> *And take away their sight!*
>
> *Whistling wind from Tonga,*
> *Blow white sand from the sea.*
> *Make these giants howl with rage*
> *While I run off and flee!*

Kumaku's words were woven with magic, and as soon as she had uttered them, the wild winds blew great plumes of black and white sand toward the shore.

The giants roared with fury as the sand filled their eyes and mouths. They stumbled about, groping wildly for Kumaku, but she was already darting away with an impish smile.

Before long, Kumaku was back at her mother's house with a coconut shell full of seawater. She offered it up sweetly as though nothing had happened, but couldn't resist an impish little giggle as her mother turned back to the cooking pot. This would certainly not be Kumaku's last escapade!

Whistling wind from Fiji, blow with all your might. Fill the giants' eyes with sand

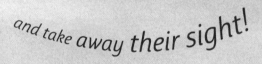

*and take away **their** sight!*

"A BASKET OF PEARS"
A story from Italy

There was once a famous tree that grew the most delicious pears. They were so good that every year, the king ordered four basketfuls. One year, however, the tree only grew enough pears to fill three and a half baskets. The harvester was afraid that the king would punish him, so he hid his daughter Perina in one of the baskets and covered her with the remaining pears so that it would appear full.

The baskets were left in the king's pantry and ignored. After a while, the little girl became hungry and began to eat the pears. A servant noticed the shrinking pile and went to look inside. She shrieked when she saw two bright eyes looking up at her!

Perina became a kitchen maid. She was cheerful and patient, and could always make people smile. Unfortunately, Perina's good character made the other maids envious. They made up a spiteful story, claiming that she had bragged about being able to steal the treasure of the witches. It was common knowledge that this chest of jewels existed, but nobody had succeeded in finding it.

When the king heard of this, he sent for Perina immediately and asked to see the treasure. She tried to explain about the lie, but the king was a hateful man and refused to believe her. "Do not return to this palace until the treasure is in your hand," he snapped.

Perina began to walk, feeling downcast. She passed an apple tree, followed by a peach tree, and finally a pear tree, which she decided to sleep in for the night. In the morning, she woke to find an old woman peering up at her. When Perina told her sorry tale, the lady took pity on her and gave her three pounds each of grease, bread, and millet along with some words of advice for her journey.

Perina went on her way and presently came upon a bakery. To her surprise, she noticed that the women were sweeping the oven with their own hair. *What can I give them to help?* she wondered, and then remembered the millet. She gave the women all of it, and the ears of millet became a very good broom when tied together.

All of a sudden, Perina heard vicious barks – two huge dogs were racing toward her with frightening ferocity. She began to run, but they were almost upon her. Searching frantically in her basket, she grabbed the loaves of bread and hurled them at the dogs. To her utter relief, they stopped in their tracks and started eating while she crept away.

As Perina walked, a glittering stream began to trickle along beside her. Gradually, it became a wide river, and Perina noticed that its color had changed to a disturbing blood red. Her path came to an end, and the old woman's words of advice echoed in her mind. *When you reach the red river and can go no further, you must utter these words:*

> *Wondrous river running red,*
> *I must find a way through.*
> *Make a path between your banks,*
> *And I'll walk over you.*

As soon as Perina had uttered these words, the river divided, allowing her to hop down and walk between two walls of water. On the other side of the bank was a beautiful castle belonging to the witches. Its enormous front door was being opened and slammed shut by some magical force.

Gingerly, Perina approached and rubbed the grease she had been given onto its hinges. Right away the door slowed and swung open.

On a table in the hall sat a wooden chest. *This must be the treasure*, Perina thought, and took it in her arms.

As Perina ran out of the castle, she was horrified to hear the chest shout, "Door – kill her!"

"I certainly shall not," replied the door. "She was the first kind person to give my poor hinges attention for many a long year."

Perina hurried on to the river, but the chest cried, "River – drown this girl!"

"No, I won't!" said the river. "She called me 'wondrous'!"

On Perina ran until she came upon the two dogs.

"Dogs – devour her!" commanded the chest.

"No way," said the dogs. "This sweet girl gave us two loaves of bread."

When Perina came to the bakery, the chest shrieked, "Oven, burn her!"

"She'll go nowhere near this oven!" shouted the women. "That millet she gave us prevents us from tearing out our own hair."

Perina was almost back at the king's castle and couldn't resist peeking into the chest. Out hopped a hen with a brood of golden chicks, but before she could blink, they disappeared! Perina tried desperately to find them and arrived back at the same pear tree. The old woman was still there with the hen and chicks pecking around her. At her command, they hopped back into the open chest.

At last, Perina arrived back at the castle.
As she approached, the king's son whispered
in her ear, "When my father asks you
to name your reward, ask for the chest
of coal in the cellar."

A crowd began to gather as Perina presented the king
with the witch's treasure. He opened the chest and
out jumped the hen and her chicks. The king
roared with laughter.
   "Perina, you have excelled yourself.
Now, name your reward!"
   "I would like a chest of coal,
Your Majesty," she said.

A murmur traveled around the
crowd, and eyebrows were raised.
   "Ha ha ha! You shall have it.
Bring up the coal chest!" roared
the king.

The coal chest arrived, and when
it opened, out leaped the prince!
   "Now you may marry my
son, if you wish," said the
king, smiling grandly.

But Perina wasn't at all
sure that she did wish to
be married. She was ready
for more adventures!

"THE SHINING DRAGONS"

A story from Lesotho

Thakáne and her brothers were orphans. Since their father, a famous chief, had died, she had become a mother to her brothers. She ground their corn, cooked their meat, and gathered water for them from the spring.

The time came for Thakáne's brothers to go to Tribal School. Traditionally, the boys would have been picked up after five months by their father and presented with a new set of clothes, weapons, and shields. As their father was no longer alive, this task fell to Thakáne.

When five months had passed, Thakáne arrived and gave her brothers the clothes she had worked so hard to make, but they turned their noses up at them.

"These clothes are not fit for the sons of a famous chief! We need blankets, hip cloths,and caps made from animal skins. And most importantly, we need shields made from the hide of a *nanabolele*, one of the fearsome dragons who lives underwater and whose skin shines like the Moon and stars on a dark night."

Thakáne threw her hands up indignantly, "And how do you expect me to find this fearsome dragon?"

"You'll just have to find a way. We'd rather stay and rot in these huts than leave Tribal School with the same clothes as everyone else. Father would never have allowed that to happen."

Thakáne couldn't bear to feel that she had somehow failed her father, however unfair the accusations. With a hardened expression, she returned to the village and called a meeting.

"Villagers, I have a dangerous mission to undertake, and I ask for your help. Would the bravest and strongest among you be prepared to help me find and slay one of the *nanabolele*?"

A murmur of apprehension rolled around the room like wind in the grass. Some questioned Thakáne's suitability for the mission, but others saw how determined she was and agreed to help her.

The following day, Thakáne led a group of the bravest villagers on a quest to find and slay a dragon. They trekked under the baking Sun, past elephants wallowing in waterholes and giraffes sedately munching on leaves. Eventually, they came to a wide stream.
   "It looks deep," Thakáne said. "Perhaps the *nanabolele* are in here."
Then she began to sing:

> *Come on out, you nanabolele;*
> *I have need of you.*
> *My brothers want your shining skin,*
> *And nothing else will do!*

As soon as her song had finished, the water of the stream began to swirl and heave. The party drew back in fear, but only a frog leaped out!

After several weeks of walking, they reached the final river. It was wider than all the others. Thakáne threw a piece of meat into the water. The group watched and waited, but nothing happened. Thakáne sang her song, but still the water did not move. She threw more meat into the water, but the surface of the river didn't so much as ripple.
   "Come on, Thakáne," somebody called out. "We're never going to find the dragons, and we're tired. It's time to go back to the village."

But Thakáne wasn't convinced and begged the group for one final attempt. She killed an ox and threw its body into the river, then sang again with all her might. This time the water began to move, but there was no dragon or frog. Instead, an old woman appeared. She beckoned to the villagers with a wizened hand before disappearing below the water. At once, Thakáne and the rest of the company dove in after her.

They swam down a long way. As soon as their feet touched the bottom, the villagers realized that the river was enchanted, because they were able to breathe normally. They found themselves standing among a cluster of huts. It was eerie; there were no children running around, and no adults talking or cooking. The village was deserted.

"Alas, it didn't used to be like this," said the old woman sadly. "There was a time when these huts were full, and the village was alive with the sounds of people going about their daily business."
"What happened to them?" asked Thakáne.
"The *nanabolele* ate them all!" said the old woman despairingly. "They only left me because I am so old and thin. They thought I would be more use working for them."

Thakáne became wary – what if the old woman had trapped them in order to give the *nanabolele* their next meal? The group was reassured, however, when the old lady led them to a deep hole in the ground and covered them with reeds. Minutes later, they heard the beating of wings in water. The *nanabolele* had returned.

Peeking through the reeds, Thakáne trembled in terror. Not one, not two, but a whole herd of dragons had landed on the riverbed. Their pearly skin shone like the Moon and stars on a dark night.
"I smell the sweet stench of human flesh," said one.

Cowering back, the villagers hardly dared to breathe as the *nanabolele* prowled around. At last, the dragons gave up and fell into a deep sleep. As soon as she heard snoring, Thakáne steeled herself and tiptoed over to the largest dragon. With a deep breath, she plunged her spear into its heart. At once, its body slumped to the ground. Thakáne looked fearfully toward the other dragons, but they remained deeply asleep. She motioned to the rest of the group, and they rushed over to help Thakáne skin it.

"I can't thank you enough," said Thakáne to the old woman. "Please take one of our oxen as a token of thanks."

"Thank you child," said the old lady. "But you and your company are now in great danger. When the other dragons find their leader dead, they will hunt you with a terrifying vengeance. Take this iron pebble – when you see clouds of red dust rise into the air, you will know that the *nanabolele* are on your trail. Throw down the pebble, and it will grow into an iron mountain that you must climb. There you will be safe."

The group set off as quickly as they could. Thakáne checked constantly over her shoulder to see if the red clouds were rising. Sure enough, before long, plumes of scarlet dust became visible. Thakáne threw the iron pebble down. It began to grow, but before it became too high, the group jumped on top of it and were carried up, up into the sky.

Far below, the herd of dragons arrived at the base of the iron mountain. It was very steep and slippery, and try as they might, the dragons couldn't climb it. At last, weary and frustrated, the *nanabolele* fell into a deep sleep. As soon as they began to snore, the iron mountain shrank down again, allowing the villagers to flee onward. They ran until their breath was ragged, but the red dust clouds were rising once more. The dragons had awakened!

Just in time, the group reached the village and hid in their huts, while Thakáne called the dogs together. It wasn't long before the *nanabolele* arrived, but the dogs were waiting for them. Miraculously, after one look at the snarling dogs, the tired dragons took flight!

Thakáne made the dragon skin into the shields and clothes that her brothers had asked for. She found the boys where she had left them, sulking in their huts. When Thakáne held up the radiantly shining clothes, their sullen expressions soon melted away. No one had ever worn clothes made from the hide of a *nanabolele* before, and Thakáne was rewarded for her bravery with a hundred cows.

At night, her hut glowed softly from within, for Thakáne had allowed herself a small memento from her adventure.... On the bed lay a special blanket that shone like the Moon and stars on a dark night.

Their **pearly skin** shone

like the Moon and stars on a dark night.

"WOODLAND DANCERS"
A story from the Czech Republic

Betushka and her mother lived in a tiny cottage on the edge of the woods. They were very poor; except for the cottage, all they owned were two nanny goats. It was Betushka's job to take care of them. Every day, she skipped into the woods with the goats, holding a basket containing flax fibers, a spindle, and a slice of bread for lunch.

Betushka was a happy, carefree girl. She loved to sing and dance, but she knew that her mother relied on her help spinning the flax into yarn. While the goats wandered, Betushka sat under a tree, twisting her spindle and turning the pile of flax into fine, strong yarn. As she worked, she sang out to the woods, and the twittering birds replied.

At lunchtime, Betushka went looking for ripe berries to go with her dry bread. When she returned to the clearing, Betushka spent time singing and dancing. After a short while, she reminded herself that her mother would be upset if she didn't return home with a full spindle of yarn, and sat back down again to continue to spin.

One afternoon, Betushka stood up to dance and found herself faced with a radiant maiden. She wore a white silk dress and had long, golden hair. On her head she wore a beautiful wreath of wildflowers.
  "Hello, Betushka. Do you like to dance?"

The maiden's voice was gentle, with tones of the whispering wind, the tinkling brook, and the twittering birds.
"Why, yes, I do," answered Betushka in wonder.
"Come, then," said the maiden, and she placed an arm around Betushka's waist and started to dance with her.

Their dancing was accompanied by the most entrancing music Betushka had ever heard. When she looked up, she saw a choir of birds crowded on the branches above her. They all wore tiny blue waistcoats and produced a warbling symphony of sound.

Betushka and the maiden danced for hours, without a care. Time wore on, and as the golden fingers of the Sun slipped beneath the horizon, the maiden disappeared as suddenly as she had arrived. Betushka stood dazed – had she been dreaming? No, there were the goats, and there was her basket with the half-empty spindle.
 "Oh, no!" said Betushka. "The spindle! Oh, Mother will be so upset."

Dejectedly, she made her way back to the little cottage. It was so unusual for Betushka to walk in silence that her mother ran out when she heard her footsteps. "Betushka, what's wrong? Are you unwell?"
 "No, Mother," she answered. "I'm just tired from all the singing I've been doing this afternoon."

When her mother's back was turned, she hid the basket with the spindle and unspun flax, knowing that she had one more day before her mother started spinning it. *Tomorrow I will take no notice of the maiden if she comes back*, Betushka thought to herself. *I'll spin double the amount I normally do, and Mother will never know.*

The following day, Betushka worked as hard as she could and did not go looking for berries at lunchtime. She munched her bread quickly, and when one of the goats butted its head against her affectionately, she said sadly, "No, my dear, I mustn't dance today."
 "Why mustn't you?"
Betushka started with surprise – it was the whispering, tinkling, twittering voice of the maiden. Nervously, she replied, "Yesterday when we danced I forgot all about my spinning, and today I must spin double to make up for it."
 "Don't you worry about that," said the maiden. "We'll get your spinning done. Now, come and dance with me!"

How could Betushka refuse? Up she jumped, and the two began their

dance all over again. They pirouetted and skipped while the choir of birds sang joyfully. As the golden hour faded into twilight, the maiden ceased the dance and grabbed the pile of flax. She attached the fibers to a tree and turned the spindle so fast that it became a blur of movement. In minutes, the spindle was fully loaded with yarn.

When Betushka arrived home, her mother was angry and wanted to know where the yarn from yesterday was.
  "Don't be upset, Mother – look how much I have today!"
  "Humph," responded her mother and stumped off to milk the goats.

The next morning, Betushka willed the time to pass. At last, lunchtime came, and Betushka stood in the clearing expectantly. Sure enough, the maiden appeared, and the two danced with such grace and elegance that it seemed as though their feet hardly touched the ground. The birds sang even more sweetly, and Betushka was filled with such happiness she could hardly bear it.

As evening fell, Betushka finally noticed the world around her. She scolded herself for forgetting the spindle again, but this time, the maiden did not help her spin. Instead, she asked for Betushka's basket. As soon as it was in her hand, she vanished and then reappeared.
  "Do not look in the basket until you arrive home," the maiden cautioned, and with that, she disappeared.

Betushka wanted to obey the maiden, but the basket felt so light. What if she had been tricked? Surely if she just peeked in.... Betushka lifted the cloth covering, only to find a pile of birch leaves! She cried bitter tears and threw a handful of the leaves away in anger.

Betushka dawdled the rest of the way, afraid to arrive home and be faced with her mother's wrath. Before she had entered the gate to their little dwelling, Betushka's mother ran out.
  "What did you do to that spindle yesterday?" she asked.

Reddening, Betushka shook her head dumbly.

"I started reeling the yarn on my spinning wheel today, but no matter how much I reeled, the spindle remained quite full. I cried out in disbelief, blaming evil spirits, and all of a sudden, the spindle was empty!" said Betushka's mother.

Betushka burst into tears and admitted everything to her mother.

"Oh, Betushka, why didn't you tell me so? The maiden you danced with was a wood maiden! They come out at midday and midnight, and they like to dance with little children and give them presents."

On hearing this, Betushka ran to uncover the basket once more. It was still full of leaves, but they were not birch.... Betushka shrieked with excitement. As she and her mother leaned over the basket, their faces glowed yellow. The leaves had been turned to gold!

With these riches, Betushka's mother could buy a farm with enough land for the goats and a few cattle, too. Betushka no longer needed to spend her days spinning, and she and her mother lived comfortably.

93

Often, Betushka found herself thinking of the wood maiden longingly. She would venture back to the clearing, hoping to catch sight of her again. But the wood maiden had moved on, ready to delight and dance with another little girl or boy.

"WELL AT THE WORLD'S END"
A story from Spain

Once upon a time, there lived a king and queen with three sons – Diego, Fernando, and Pedro. It was during the wedding of their eldest son, Pedro, that tragedy struck....

The king was walking on the grounds of the palace when he heard a strange crowing from overhead. As he looked up to see a large flock of exotic birds, something fell into his eyes. He rubbed them furiously, but when he tried to open his eyes, he could only see gray, blurry shapes. After just a few days, his world had turned to darkness.

A parade of doctors, healers, herbalists, and soothsayers came to the palace, intending to cure the king of his blindness. None was successful, and the fog that had afflicted the king's sight seemed to hang mournfully over the palace and indeed the whole kingdom.

The last person to see the king was an old hermit, who lived alone in a cave in the far reaches of the kingdom. He was known for his wisdom and prophecies and gave the king some advice:
  "Someone must travel to the end of the world to find the magic well. It is full of life-giving water. Just a few drops will be enough to cure your blindness. But be warned! The well is guarded by a cunning enchantress. So far, no one has ever made the journey home...."

The king's sons all offered to make the journey, feeling sure that they would succeed where others had failed. Diego was chosen to make the journey first. He packed two small saddlebags and set off.

To reach the end of the world, one must travel very far. Diego and his steed galloped across wide plains, through dry deserts, lush forests, tall mountains, and over rushing rivers.

95

They trudged through snow and ice, baked themselves in scorching heat, and got drenched by relentless rain.

After many moons, Diego reached the sea. The only living soul around was an old fisherman. Diego approached him and asked if he knew where the Water of Life might be found.

"Indeed I do, young sir," said the fisherman. "There is a rock far out to sea. On that rock sits a castle, and in that castle is a courtyard that houses a well. In there you will find the precious Water of Life. But be careful – the well is guarded by an enchantress, who has turned many before you into stone! I advise you to go no further."

Diego would not hear of this and said angrily, "Do you realize how far I have come to find this well? At last it seems within reach, and you tell me to turn back? No enchantress will get the better of me!"

"Very well, sir," said the fisherman. "I will row you over there. But you can't say I didn't warn you!"

Diego and the fisherman set sail. The sea was as still as a lake, and it didn't take long to arrive at the rocky outcrop. As soon as the fisherman had moored the boat, Diego sprung onto the rocks. After hours of climbing he arrived, hot and exhausted, at the gates of a majestic castle. Diego entered the gates and spotted the well immediately. It was carved from dazzling white marble, and a fountain of clear water rose from its center; Diego was transfixed. Music seemed to be coming from the well, echoing up from its depths. He walked toward it as though in a trance and drew out his flask, but he was no longer alone....

A young woman stood in front of him. Her green eyes glittered like emeralds, and when she smiled, the rest of the world became blurred.

"Young man, why the hurry? You've journeyed all the way to the end of the world and must be in need of a rest and some sustenance."

"I-I'm sorry," Diego stammered. "I must– I mean– I should be leaving." As he spoke, a heaving table of food and drink appeared. The woman motioned to a velvet couch with plump cushions.

"You wouldn't leave me to eat alone, would you?"

Taking her outstretched hand, Diego sat down and began to eat. Hardly had the first bite touched his lips when he was overcome by drowsiness. Before he could utter a word, the poor prince had been turned to stone. Of course, the young woman was really the enchantress. With a snap of her fingers, she ordered her servants to take the statue of Diego down to the castle's cellar.

After a year, the Royal Family despairingly gave up hope of Diego ever returning, and they turned to Fernando. He set off with just as much optimism as Diego, but a year passed with no news, and the king and queen asked Pedro, the eldest, to make the journey.

"See you soon, Mother and Father. I won't let you down," said Pedro confidently as he rode off.

Another year went by, and Pedro did not return. The king and queen were beside themselves. Not only was the king still blind, but they had lost all three of their dear sons.

Valentina was Pedro's wife. She went to see the king and queen and begged them to let her try the journey. The king and queen refused, but this did not deter her – she always did exactly as she pleased.

In the dead of night, Valentina dressed in a suit of her husband's clothes and rode like the wind. She spent many days and nights galloping across the lands until she found herself on a bleak and barren shore. An old man stood gazing thoughtfully out to sea. Valentina spoke in the gruffest voice she could muster.

"Good day, fisherman. Can you tell me how to reach the well at the end of the world?"

The fisherman shook his head sadly. "I have rowed three young men like yourself to yonder island in the last three years. None has returned. I won't make the journey again."

Valentina decided to tell the old man everything. She explained that she was really a woman, and that her husband was one of the princes who had come before her. The fisherman nodded gravely.

"The enchantress is able to fool the hearts of men, but perhaps she will not be able to overcome you so easily."

Before long, Valentina was entering the gates of the castle. She soon heard the well's haunting melody and ran quickly toward the crystal fountain. Having filled her flask with the Water of Life, she ventured inside the castle. A small wooden door lay ajar. Valentina pushed it open and went down the stone steps.

She stood for a moment, allowing her eyes to adjust to the gloom. The room was crowded with stone statues. Suddenly, something caught her eye – one of the statues looked familiar.... Valentina walked over to it and gasped in fright. It was her dear husband, Pedro!

"Can I help you?" asked a sharp voice.
Valentina turned to see a pretty young woman.

"I think you must be lost, sir," said the woman. "Allow me to take you back up to the castle for a hearty meal."

But Valentina was prepared, and these charms had no effect on her. She stepped forward with a hand on her sword. At once, the young woman melted into a hunched old lady and put out a quavering hand.

"Please, sir, have mercy on an old woman."
Valentina drew the sword with a flourish, and the old woman transformed into a haughty queen.

"You wouldn't dare attack a royal queen," she said.
But Valentina did dare; she stepped quickly forward and plunged her sword into the queen's heart.
Instantly, the witch turned to dust, and hundreds of stone statues sprang to life.

After a joyful reunion, Valentina and the princes filled their flasks with the Water of Life. Triumphantly, they returned home and presented the king with the healing water.

Tearfully, and filled with happiness, the king embraced his family.
"Thank you, my sons, for undertaking this adventure on my behalf. But thank you most of all to my bold Valentina. There is no one braver in the whole kingdom, and you shall wear the crown once I am gone."

Queen Valentina became a ruler of great fairness, and while she listened calmly to any advice given to her, in the end, she always did exactly as she pleased.

"THE WINGED MONSTER"
A Native American story

There was once a time when humans were haunted by spirits and terrorized by monsters. These demons couldn't bear the light of the Sun and would stay hidden in caves during the daylight hours. At nighttime they would rear their ugly heads and roam the lands, searching for innocent humans to devour.

The most fearsome of all was the Winged Monster. It had no body or legs, just an enormous head that was covered with dark, tangled fur. Its eyes flashed with venomous cruelty, its sharp teeth gnashed furiously, and on either side of its cheeks grew two huge, feathered wings. The monster loved to soar through the sky, searching for unsuspecting victims.

One night, a young boy saw the Winged Monster not far from his camp while he was collecting firewood. Running as fast as he could, he went to warn his people. As soon as they heard the news, everyone fled, leaving just one woman named Yodagent with her baby.

Yodagent was fed up with having to run off every time somebody spotted a monster and decided not to stand for it any longer. She was a brave woman, and her reasoning was this: since no one else was prepared to stand up to this demon, she might as well do it herself.

Yodagent sat close to the fire in her wigwam, stoking the flames higher and higher until the blaze was roaring. She then added a handful of stones to the red-hot heart of the fire. Having done this, Yodagent sat back and waited for the Winged Monster, calmly rocking her baby while singing a soft lullaby.

All at once, a shadow loomed in the doorway of her wigwam. The monster leered greedily at her with eyes glowing red.

It flapped a pair of leathery wings, and rows of horrible fangs glinted in the moonlight. Brave Yodagent stayed perfectly composed, acting as though she hadn't noticed the Winged Monster. She pretended that she was cooking a meal.

"Mmm, how delicious!" Yodagent said loudly.

Using a large fork, she picked up one hot stone after another, and pretended to put them into her mouth.

"My goodness, I have never tasted food like this!" Yodagent continued, pretending that the piping-hot rocks were really slabs of delectable meat.

Hearing her words, the Winged Monster was beside itself with greed. It swooped through the open door and went straight for the pile of rocks hissing in the fire, thinking they were fresh meat. The Winged Monster opened its enormous jaws wide and snatched up the rocks, gulping them down before it could register what they were.

Clutching her baby tightly to her chest, Yodagent moved to the back of her wigwam as a piercing howl of rage and pain escaped from the Winged Monster. It flapped its giant wings and flew from the village. Yodagent watched as it disappeared over the hills with bloodcurdling shrieks, leaving a trail of thick steam in its wake.

She went back into her wigwam and started to cook some real strips of meat on the fire. Yodagent took great pleasure in saying loudly, "Eat rocks if you like, but I prefer to eat real meat!"

This time, no dark shadow graced her doorway; the Winged Monster was never seen again.

BEYOND THE FAIRY TALE

Background to the Stories

"Aurora and the Giants," Germany
The German Brothers Grimm are famous for their fairy tale collections, published in the early 1800s. Most of the tales they recorded were related to them by women, passed down through generations.

"The Black Bull," Scotland
In medieval times, belief in fairies and supernatural beings was common. Some of the Scottish fairy tales handed down to us were originally related as true stories!

"The Magic Boxes," Iran
In Classical Iran (originally Persia), storytelling was an important part of culture and entertainment. Professional storytellers would perform to audiences in a variety of places: from royal courts to coffee houses and the tents of nomadic people.

"Spirits of the Dead," Nigeria
This tale comes from the Yoruba people, whose folktales often involve singing and dancing. The Egungun still play an important part in Yoruba culture. They are celebrated every year with a festival during which people dress up in the kinds of costumes described in the story.

"The Wandering Harpist," Russia
Between the 11th and 17th centuries in Russia, entertainers were known as *skomorokhi*. They sang, danced, told stories, and played music. The stringed *gusli* was popular at this time. It is thought to be one of the oldest musical instruments in Russia.

"The Songs of Liu," China
Singing is an all-important part of Yao culture. People tell stories with songs and use them for all kinds of occasions, from feasting and declaring love to relaxing and even working.

"Sacred Waterfall," North America
This Native American story comes from a tribe called the Onguiaahra. They lived on the Niagara Peninsula and gained a reputation for being a peaceful people.

"The Tiger and the Jackal," India
India has a very rich storytelling heritage and is sometimes called the home of the fairy tale. Stories crossed the world with traders and travelers, which may explain why many Asian and European fairy tales have similar themes.

"The Company of Elves," Scotland
The fairies left behind a legacy of place names in Scotland. The country is peppered with hills, glens, and mountains that have been named after the "wee folk" (fairy beings).

"Maru-me and the Wrestler," Japan
During the time of the emperors, sumo wrestling was official entertainment for the royal court. The sport has ancient associations with religion, and some rituals are still practiced today, such as throwing salt in the ring to purify it before a match. Sumo wrestling is thought to be one of the oldest organized sports in the world.

"Goddess of the Sun," Mexico
This tale comes from the Aztecs, who ruled a large empire in Mexico in the 15th and 16th centuries. They believed that the world had been created and destroyed four times. The story of the Sun Goddess relates to the world we currently live in – the fifth age of Earth.

"Bella and the Bear," Sweden
Forests are often used as the backdrop for fairy tales, filled with talking animals and mythical beings. From the very beginning, their deep, dark interiors and shadowy trees have aroused a sense of magic and mystery.

"The Snake King," Siberia
This story was told by the Altai people of Siberia. They are a nomadic tribe who have always respected and lived in harmony with nature.

"The Fairy Hill," England
Mounds and hills were commonly thought to be the homes of fairies in the British Isles. Other signs that fairies had been active were fairy rings – circles of mushrooms that were thought to signify that a fairy dance had taken place.

"The Coconut Shell," Fiji
Music has always been a hugely important part of Fijian culture. Their traditional performance, called the *meke*, involves telling stories and legends through dancing, singing, and clapping. To this day, the *meke* remains Fiji's most famous national art.

"A Basket of Pears," Italy
The Italian tradition of storytelling began in places where groups of people commonly gathered, in both public and family settings. Crowds would form to hear tales of magic and adventure. These stories were also popular on long journeys and pilgrimages.

"The Shining Dragons," Lesotho
This tale comes from the Sotho people, known for their folktales and praise poems. Traditionally, they were told dramatically – spectators joining with performers to chant, clap, and tell the tales of their ancestors.

"Woodland Dancers," Czech Republic
Village life used to involve communal work and long periods of inactivity in the evenings. Telling stories passed the time and kept people entertained. Tales were traded by travelers, too, and might be told in return for a night at an inn.

"Well at the World's End," Spain
When wells appear in folklore, they are often associated with healing and magic. Wells used to hold an important place in communities – people would leave offerings for the gods, and wishes were made there.

"The Winged Monster," North America
This Native American story comes from the Iroquois people. Their stories are designed to teach and explain things about the world. Important life lessons are imparted to the listener alongside dramatic plot lines, brave heroes, and mythical creatures.

Talking Points

"Aurora and the Giants"
At first sight, Tertulla seems frightening. But she loves Aurora like a daughter, and Aurora looks past appearances to the kind soul within.

"The Black Bull"
Jessie may be young, but she is very determined – when obstacles are placed in her path, she refuses to give up!

"The Magic Boxes"
Have you ever felt helpless? Nazneen has moments of feeling at a loss, but her boldness and curiosity always enable her to find a way.

"Spirits of the Dead"
No one listens to Moremi, but she refuses to be deterred. She places herself in danger in order to save her village because she has a strong sense of self belief.

"The Wandering Harpist"
The czarina rescues her husband using cleverness and cunning, but she has to dress as a man to be taken seriously. Why do you think this is?

"The Songs of Liu"
Some disapprove of friendship between tribes, but Liu is popular with everyone. Her singing brings people together, and she will not be silenced!

"Sacred Waterfall"
When Willow tries to help, everyone dismisses her, but she refuses to give up on them. Sometimes bravery lies in quiet persistence rather than loud actions.

"The Tiger and the Jackal"
In many well-known fairy tales, the man rescues the woman. In this story, that stereotype is turned on its head – girls can save the day, too!

"The Company of Elves"
Everyone warns Janet about Tam Lin, but she wants to help him and withstands a variety of difficult ordeals in order to save his life. Sometimes it's better to listen to yourself and trust your own judgment over other people's.

"Maru-me and the Wrestler"
The wrestler assumes that Maru-me will be weaker than him because she is a little girl. Have you ever made an assumption about someone based on his or her gender?

"Goddess of the Sun"
Lord of Snails is arrogant, while Little Spots shows true courage. A hero is not
always the person who shouts the loudest.

"Bella and the Bear"
Have you ever done something for the pure joy of it? Bella knows that her
nanny will be upset if she wanders off, but sometimes, adventures must be had!

"The Snake King"
Altyn-Aryg is furious when her father denies her the same rights as a man.
She will not accept her fate and leaves to prove herself. Do people still think
men are better suited for leadership roles?

"The Fairy Hill"
Kate manages to save both her sister and the prince. Her heroism comes from
a strong desire to help people, and she doesn't shy away from adventure, either!

"The Coconut Shell"
Kumaku strays from the path, but she defeats giants! In the past, adventurous
boys were praised, while bold girls were frowned upon. Does this attitude
persist today?

"A Basket of Pears"
Perina has to go through a series of difficult challenges to prove her innocence.
Have you ever felt ignored or distrusted?

"The Shining Dragons"
Thakáne feels that her brothers have given her an impossible task, but she
perseveres, and her determination pays off.

"Woodland Dancers"
Betushka would go on dancing forever with the wood maiden if she could,
but all good things must come to an end.

"Well at the World's End"
Valentina's bravery was more remarkable because the three brothers
had already disappeared, so she knew she faced an ordeal.

"The Winged Monster"
Have you ever had to think on your feet? Yodagent stays calm and uses her
intelligence to defeat the Winged Monster.

Bibliography

"Aurora and the Giants"
"The Giant's Forest," in *The Queen's Mirror: Fairy Tales by German Women 1780-1900*, by Shawn Jarvis and Jeannine Blackwell. University of Nebraska Press, 2001

"The Black Bull"
"The Black Bull of Norroway," in *More English Fairy Tales*, by Joseph Jacobs. Dover, 1967

"The Magic Boxes"
"The 'Pink Pearl' Prince," in *Folk Tales of Iran*, by Asha Dhar. Sterling Publishers, 1978

"Spirits of the Dead"
"Moremi and the Egunguns," in *Tales of Yoruba Gods and Heroes*, by Harold Courlander. Fawcett Publications Inc., 1973

"The Wandering Harpist"
"The Tsaritsa Harpist," in *Russian Folk-Tales*, translated by Leonard A. Magnus. E.P. Dutton and Co., 1916

"The Songs of Liu"
"Maiden Liu, the Songster," in *Chinese Folktales*, by Louise Kuo and Yuan His. Celestial Arts, 1976

"Sacred Waterfall"
"Bending Willow," in *American Indian Fairy Tales*, by Margaret Compton. Abela Publishing, 2009

"The Tiger and the Jackal"
"The Farmer's Wife and the Tiger," in *The Magic Umbrella and Other Stories for Telling*, compiled by Eileen Cowell. David McCay, 1976

"The Company of Elves"
"Tamlane," in *More English Fairy Tales*, by Joseph Jacobs. Dover, 1967

"Maru-me and the Wrestler"
Three Strong Women: a Tale from Japan, by Claus Stamm. Viking, 1990

"Goddess of the Sun"
"The Fifth Sun," in *Stories told by the Aztecs*, by Carleton Beals Abelard. Schuman, 1970

"Bella and the Bear"
"Bella's Glorious Adventure," in *Swedish Folk Tales,* by Helena Nyblom. Floris Books, 2004

"The Snake King"
"Altyn-Aryg," in *Siberian and other Folk-Tales,* by C. Fillingham Coxwell. The C.W. Daniel Company, 1925

"The Fairy Hill"
"Kate Crackernuts," in *English Fairy Tales,* by Joseph Jacobs. Everymans, 1993

"The Coconut Shell"
"Kumaku and the Giant," in *Myths and Legends of Fiji and Rotuma,* by A.W. Reed and Inez Hames. A.H. and A.W. Reed, 1967

"A Basket of Pears"
"The Little Girl Sold with the Pears," in *Italian Folktales,* by Italo Calvino. Houghton Mifflin Harcourt, 1992

"The Shining Dragons"
"Nanabole, Who Shines in the Light," in *Tales from the Basotho,* by Minnie Postma. University of Texas Press, 1974

"Woodland Dancers"
"The Wood Fairy," in *Favorite Fairy Tales Told in Czechoslovakia,* by Virginia Haviland. Little, Brown, 1966

"Well At The World's End"
"The Princess Who Went to the End of the Earth," in *Spanish Fairy Tales,* translated by Vera Gissing. Hamyln, 1973

"The Winged Monster"
"The Brave Woman and the Flying Head," in *Iroquois Stories: Heroes and Heroines, Monsters and Magic,* by Joseph Bruchac. Crossing, 1995

"After nourishment,
shelter, and companionship,
stories are the thing we need
most in the world."

— Philip Pullman

THE
END